A Time And A Place

by

Karl Bullock

with
Amy Bul ock

A Time And A Place
Copyright 2024 by Karl W. Bullock
First Edition, First Printing

ISBN 979-8-218-97281-3

Updates on publication of this book and others may be found on OpenPortalBooks.com.

You can email the author at karl@openportalbooks.com

Dedicated to our Daughters
Carly and Lindsay
(our "Kelly" and "Katie")

PROLOGUE

Robert realized he was staring with his mouth open. He'd seen and heard the man who was speaking on several occasions, but he'd never heard him speak in a language he could understand. Yet, here he was, addressing the assembled crowd in perfect mid-western English. Robert didn't even know the man's name.

The speech was very enlightening, but that was not what Robert needed to talk to him about. As soon as he was finished, Robert made his way through the crowd and waited in line for the others who were talking to him. Finally, his time in line came, and the look on the man's face was one of recognition. This was not surprising, because Robert had been all but stalking this man and his friends for the last several days.

"I have a problem that only you can help me with," Robert finally said. The man was obviously taken aback, because he'd never heard Robert speak in a language he understood before today either.

As they spoke back and forth, it became obvious by the expressions on the man's face that a solution was not likely. The time they had was shorter than Robert would have liked, but because of those crowded around waiting their turn, he understood. Robert's hope faded as the reality of the situation set in.

"Well, I understand if you can't help," Robert finally said, obviously exasperated. "I just don't know what to do next!"

The look on the man's face turned very compassionate, and that calmed Robert down a bit. Suddenly, there was an expression of apparent inspiration on the man's face, and he said, "I do have a suggestion for you, but I cannot tell you exactly what it means."

"Tell me! I need to have some direction!" Robert pleaded.

"This is my suggestion," said the man. "Go to where it all began."

Robert's face just froze in a "*what does that mean?*" expression.

The man softened his voice and said again, more slowly, "Go to where it all began. That is where you will find your answer."

One of the other members of the group came up and said something to the man, upon which he then turned back around to Robert and said, "I apologize, but this is the only suggestion I have for you, my friend. We will, however, be praying for your plight. Please, if you will excuse me, I have many others to attend to," and with that, the man clasped his hands on the Robert's shoulders and looked compassionately into the Robert's eyes and gave him a parting smile. Then the man turned around to the others waiting for him.

Robert just turned and left, still pondering what he had just been told. "*Go to where it all began*," he whispered to himself, confused as to just what that meant.

What happened to him over the next several hours just became another series of events that only one other man who had ever lived would understand – and unfortunately, *that* man had just been murdered.

CHAPTER 1

Dr. Ned Welch had been working on this project now for two years, and while much had been accomplished, there was much more to process. He was one of the principle directors in an ongoing archaeological project in the old part of the city of Jerusalem. Over the years there had been hundreds of these such projects, and they were becoming increasingly difficult not only because of the sensitivity of the area, but because of the close proximity of everyday life in both the ancient and the modern cities. In this case, it had started innocuously enough when two children playing near an old abandoned building discovered a metal rod protruding out of the ground in a deep hole near one of the corners of the building, and were making a game out of attempting to pull it out of the ground. They had loosened it enough that they were sure it should just pull out, when suddenly, one of the boys decided to give it a hard jerk. As he fell back the rod came with him, along with a long, very ragged rope attached to the other end of the rod. Apparently, the larger end of the rod had been fashioned into sort of an eyelet where the rope had been tied. As they pulled it out, they became increasingly aware that the rope was not only very old, out it looked ancient.

Thankfully, they had showed it to one of their parents who instantly recognized it as something he'd seen in nearby museums.

The resulting chain of events had led to the excavation, and Dr. Welch and his team had begun the process of finding out just what the boys had uncovered. In the process they had extracted a number of artifacts that appeared to be around the first or second centuries. Their site plans were constantly updated as they discovered more of the remains long since buried beneath the abandoned building and the surrounding areas. Because of the denseness of the area, obtaining the necessary permissions to begin excavation had been lengthy, and they were necessarily limited in the scope of the project, but this was always a concern in any settled area.

Ned was pouring over charts of the excavated area when an assistant came up.

"Dr. Welch, I think you may want to see this."

He led Ned over to an area that had been opened up into a small cavern embedded in the ground. One of his associates also came over just as one of the workers climbed out of the work area with one of the burlap bags the workers used to transport items found during excavation. As he stood before Ned and those assembled around him, he opened the bag and inside were several coins and what apparently had once been a small pouch made of some sort of animal skin with a somewhat crude drawstring. It was in rough shape, so Ned took it carefully over to a table they used to clean items retrieved from the excavations. He placed the items on a heavy white paper and digital photographs were taken from several angles. Then Ned took a brush and carefully cleared the dirt and other contaminates, as much as he could from one side of the pouch. Then, another set of photographs were taken. He then turned the pouch over and repeated the process, after which he moved the pouch over to another clean paper.

The drawstrings had rotted through over the centuries, and the pouch had holes in it, although some of the coins were still inside what was left of the pouch. With gloved hands, Ned separated the drawstrings that had once held the pouch closed, and very carefully emptied the remainder of the contents onto the paper. What they saw was several more coins, apparently of ancient origin. The coins were all covered with sediment and were heavily corroded, as they had likely been exposed to water over the intervening centuries.

As they separated the coins and began to sort them by size, one coin stood out from the others, and there was something familiar about it. Ned picked it up carefully, placed it in his gloved hand and held it under the magnifying glass mounted to the table. As he looked at the coin, a cold chill ran down his back, for what he saw on the edges of the coin was perfectly spaced serrated edges. Not only that, he could see that if the corrosion was cleared away, the coin would be almost perfectly round. In fact, he could swear he saw the wave of hair in the back of George Washington's head!

He looked up from the magnifying glass and said, "We need to make some phone calls!"

CHAPTER 2
Pasadena, CA

2001

Dr. Lewis Donaldson was on his way to prepare for a meeting with representatives of the U.S. Department of Education. Today's preparation was for his goal of obtaining a series of grants to study the historical effects of the Roman Empire in the first through fifth centuries, and that empire's effect ultimately on the origins of the United States. He was working on a theory he had developed that certain specific events in that period of time led directly to the establishment of the United States. To make his case he would need to do extensive research, including excursions to Italy, Germany, and the Middle East, and he needed funding for necessary travel and expenses.

His first stop today would be Lydia Buchwald's office in the Caltech Administration building. Lydia was his grant coordinator, and she was responsible for helping him through the grant applications process, and once enough funds were approved, her office would manage the receiving and expending of the funds. It was not lost on anyone involved that obtaining grants for history research would be a feather in Caltech's hat, and would bolster their Humanities/Social Sciences Department. Lydia's staff would be critical for his grant application and the management of the funds once granted, and she was well respected in her field as well.

As he pulled up to a stoplight on the way, his mind was racing through all the things he wanted to accomplish with this grant, as well as the application process itself. But as he waited for the light to change, something caught his attention across the street on the other side of the stoplight. It was a large Protestant Church that took up an entire block. On Sundays there was always a small traffic jam here at lunch as the congregation exited, and each member headed their separate ways, which caused Lewis no small annoyance, since that's roughly the time he came through each Sunday on his way to eat lunch with his daughter. Many times their meal began with her getting an earful about how deluded all these people were and all the money and time they were wasting worshiping a god who didn't exist.

You see, Lewis Donaldson was an atheist, and he was proud of it. He'd spent his life arguing against not only the Bible, but against any religion that claimed to answer to a higher power. In his mind, there was no higher power. We were on our own. But, at least he was honest about what that meant. If we were to survive as a species, we had to be ever vigilant not to destroy ourselves. If there was no 'master plan' and, of course, no 'master planner', then all options were open, including our ability to end all life on earth with impunity. Logically, then, he was an anti-military, anti-war, anti-nuke activist, and he held those beliefs forth in his philosophy and the courses he taught, and was well-respected in the communities of those with similar beliefs.

A professor of history at Caltech, "Lew", as his friends called him, was also the definition of an absent-minded professor. That not only amused his friends and colleagues, but it served to endear him to his students. Forty nine years old, he and his wife

5

had separated a little more than two years earlier and she had moved to the east coast with their son, ostensibly to care for her ill and aging parents. Their relationship was still cordial and while he missed having someone at home, he had grown used to living pretty much on his own, though his daughter stayed in California with him and had started her own business. With longish dark brown hair and intense blue eyes, Lew had worked hard to have a 'professor-ly' look, and had achieved exactly that. His work had always been in the classroom, and he looked the part.

His thought processes were disrupted by the blare of a car horn behind him, and it took him a second to realize the light had changed and the folks behind him were not very interested in sitting through another one. So, on he went.

He arrived at the campus and went straight to Lydia's office. As he entered, her student assistant was sitting at the desk in the outer office.

"Good Morning, Dr. Donaldson. What can we do for you?" she asked.

"Is Lydia in?"

"Yes. Let me see if she's free."

She went into Lydia's office just as she was just finishing up a call. When she hung up she saw her assistant and raised here eyebrows in a 'what?' expression.

"Dr. Donaldson's here to see you," her assistant said.

"Really?" she asked with a bit of amusement, then with a wry look almost whispered, "Is he wearing socks this time?"

"Yes," the girl giggled, "and they actually match today!"

Lydia flashed a knowing grin and said, "Send him in, then."

In a few seconds Lew came through her door.

"Morning, Lew. What can I do for you?"

"Well, I just want to make sure we have everything ready for the meeting at lunch on the 10th. Is there anything else that needs to be done before then?"

Lydia screwed up her face, cocked her head a bit, then said, "Well, actually no. Everything is ready. You do realize *today* is the 10th, don't you?"

Lew had a somewhat confused look on his face. He looked down where his wristwatch would be, realizing too late that he'd left it at home – again – so he just smiled and said, "Oh, yes. I guess it is. So, lunch today then, right?"

Lydia chuckled and said, "Yes, lunch. Do you want me to come to your office when it's time so we can ride over to the meeting together?"

Lew shook his head. "Thanks, but no. I'll need to leave from the meeting for the conference tomorrow, so I'll just meet you there."

"OK, then," said Lydia. "I will see you there."

As he left, Lydia's assistant came back in. "That was quick." she said.

"Oh yes. Just had to remind him he'd forgotten what day it was - again. To be on the safe side, though, go down to his office when it's time for him to leave at eleven and, if necessary, remind him how to get to the restaurant. I know that man is brilliant, but I swear I sometimes wonder how he finds his way home at night."

"Well, I can state with absolute confidence it's with no help from above." They both laughed a bit too mischievously, then went back to work.

CHAPTER 3
Arlington, VA

Early 1980s

She was a vision – at least in the eyes of Tom Reed.

Tom and his team were working hard on the design for the eventual implementation of a wild idea he'd had in college while working on his Applied Physics Master's degree, an idea the military had become very interested in: The possibility of being able to make an object just 're-appear' somewhere else on earth without actually having to physically transport it. DARPA, the Defense Advanced Research Projects Administration, had recruited Tom to fully develop this possibility and, if and when the technology became available, make it happen and fund the project, so Tom had put a team together and began working on the idea. It was a daunting project, and practically none of the technology existed, so there was much work to do!

Kathy Parker had been at DARPA since graduating college a couple of years before Tom. Her function was to manage the staff of a another rather large project housed in the office space down the hall from Tom's group, and his eyes were automatically drawn to her every time he saw her.

She was one year younger than Tom, but at least a decade more mature, he thought, and rumored to be very competent at everything she did. With her brown shoulder-length hair that she would many times wear in a pony tail during work hours, she was hard to miss. He had seen her in the hallway before, generally when she was shuffling between offices, but never had conjured up the courage to say something to her. Turns out today that didn't matter, because one of the techs that worked with Tom was married to one of her friends. While they were both in the hallway chatting, Kathy appeared, said 'hello' to Tom's friend, and he immediately turned around and made Tom's day.

"Hi, Kathy," he had said as she started by. "Say, have you met my friend and lead, Tom Reed?"

Kathy stopped and turned towards Tom.

"Why no, but I've seen you around from time to time. Hi Tom. I'm Kathy Parker."

"Nice to meet you Kathy," Tom said shaking her hand. "I understand you work in the group Ted Sanderson leads."

"Yes. I've been in his group for a couple of years now. I handle the office staff and I'm generally his right hand. It's interesting work, and he's a good lead and great guy to work for."

"Yeah, I know Ted, but we've never really done anything socially outside work."

Just then the tech received a page and excused himself leaving Kathy and Tom alone in the hallway, resulting in a bit of an awkward moment, until Kathy spoke.

"So, look," she said, "I have a rather pressing deadline. How about we catch up later?"

"Sure, I'd like that," Tom said. Tell you what..." and he pulled out a business card with his office phone and pager number on it, turned it over and wrote his home phone number on the back.

9

"Give me a call when you have some free time and I shall treat you to a sumptuous meal.....something better than burgers and fries," and smiled his best 'I'm really cool' smile.

"Do you have another one of those?" she asked.

"Sure," and he pulled out another one. She took it and wrote her number on the back.

"Here's my number. I suspect your hours are weirder than mine, so when you have some free time, why don't you just call me? And, I'm OK with burgers and fries."

Tom took the card and smiled. "You've got a deal!"

"Great. Bye," she said and headed down the hall.

"Bye, Kathy Parker!" he said, and that garnered him a smile as she did a quick look back over her shoulder. He waited until she was out of sight before returning to work. It took him a while to get his mind back on molecular physics.

The next day was Friday, and Tom finished early and had just come out of his office when he saw her coming down the hallway again.

"Hey!" Tom said, "Look, I'm about to finish up my week. Want to get something to eat when you get free?"

"Sure," she said, "but it'll be a couple of hours. Can you stand to wait that long?"

"Oh, I think I can stand it. Page me a when you're about ready to leave and I'll come by and pick you up."

"Then you have a deal. Talk to you then," she said as she turned and disappeared down the hall and into her work area.

"*Mom always said God works in mysterious ways*," Tom mumbled to myself, then headed to his car with a smile on his face.

Two hours later she paged him. Tom was in the parking lot absently-minded picking at a place on his finger, while simultaneously listening to a conversation between two local guys on his mobile Ham Radio rig when Kathy came out of the building. He turned off the radio, got out of the vehicle and motioned to Kathy who came over. He opened the passenger door like a gentleman and she slid in, he shut the door, and came around to his side and got in. Then Tom got the first question everyone asks the first time they're in his car.

"What's that? Are you a Cop?" she said, pointing to the small ham radio rig mounted just above the center console.

"No," he chuckled, "I'm a Ham Radio Operator, and that's my mobile radio. If you feel the need to run screaming into the night, now's the time."

She smiled, "No – I'll take the chance."

"Great! So, any preferences for dinner?" he asked.

"Don't tell me we're going to start off arguing about where to eat like my parents did," she said with a smirk.

"Nope. I'll let you in on a trick my parents used."

"Oh yeah? What's that?"

Tom smiled. "What do you *not* want to eat?"

She gave him a somewhat surprised look. "What do I *not* want to eat?"

"Right!" he said. "Most people are reluctant to say what they want, but practically nobody is shy about saying what they don't want. They view that as 'helping out' rather than 'being picky'. Once we both eliminate what we don't want, it's easy to pick from what's left. Saved many an argument for my parents. So, what do you not want?"

She smiled and nodded her head. "Well, I gotta say, I'm already impressed!"

11

"Wonderful. I'll call Mom in the morning," Tom said with his own smirk. "So?"

They both bounced around their negative preferences for a minute, and when it was over with, they decided on Italian. Mission accomplished!

"OK, then," Tom said. "I know this little Italian placed called Linzlow's, and I just love their pizza. I'm also friends with their keyboard player, so there'll be music!" - and with that he started up and headed towards the restaurant. They started out with the usual small talk on the way over - you know, '*how was your day?*', and '*do you enjoy the work?*' About ten minutes later they arrived and went in and began their first more or less informal 'date'.

For some reason neither was nervous. They felt comfortable together, and it was easy to let their guard down. By the end of the meal they'd exchanged the short version of their life stories, and become pretty well acquainted. She was from a small town in Texas, and Tom was from a small town in Mississippi. They'd both had high aspirations and she, like Tom, had ended up in an organization neither had anticipated, doing things she'd also never anticipated. The only trepidation Tom had the whole night was when the band began to play, and some couples began to take the dance floor. He looked over at the band, then looked at Kathy. She had also looked at the band and looked back his way at the same time.

"I don't dance," Tom said a bit nervously. She smiled and said, "Oh good! Me either!" and both had a good laugh, relieved looks on their faces.

They enjoyed the meal together and talked for nearly two hours, and finally left and he drove back over to DARPA where her little sports car was. They ended up sitting in his car talking for another hour. Finally, Kathy said it had been a long week, and she had some things to do before retiring for the night. So they said goodnight and she got in her car and drove off - giving her address to Tom before leaving. *"That might come in handy!"* Tom thought! He didn't remember much about the ride home. He was preoccupied thinking about something other than driving.

Several days and a couple of dates later, after he had finished for the day, Tom waited around after he closed up to pick up Kathy, and took her out for a casual dinner. Early in their relationship, they had touched on the issue of where this was all going.

"Well, I'm not looking to get married," Tom had said. "Oh! Me either," she had said, "so let's just keep it casual."

So, they kept it casual, but their first kiss that night as he dropped her off at her apartment should have been a warning that this was going to be anything but casual. But, that's how they left it. As time went on, though, and the relationship deepened, they both began to realize where this was going to end up, but neither was ready to admit it, even to themselves. Right now they were just enjoying each other's company. It didn't take long for that to change – for the better.

The next day was Saturday, and Tom and Kathy had decided to spend the day at the park, and maybe watch one of the softball games that was always going on, but really just to spend the day together. In the intervening time Tom had mounted his much-larger HF ham rig between the seats in his SUV, but didn't take it out before going to pick up Kathy.

"Oh, this is new!" she said as she put her seat-belt on, noticing the new rig. "What is this for, and what is that thing on the back?"

She was pointing towards that "thing" on the back, a high-frequency radio antenna that was mounted on the right rear bumper that had not been there until today. She had only been by Tom's house once, when he drove by one evening while they were together to pick up something for a friend, so she'd seen the living room and kitchen, but not much more. Though he had mentioned his hobby earlier in their relationship, it never really took hold with her since they'd had been connecting so much on other levels, but this brought it all back up. Normally Tom didn't have the larger antenna installed, using instead the smaller radio and the small whip on top of the car for local conversations, but since he had the HF rig that required it, Tom had put it back on. It was always another of those conversation starters.

"You remember my telling you I'm a Ham Radio operator? We never really talked about that again. This," he said pointing to the rig, "is a what's called a 'high-frequency transceiver'. It is basically a shortwave transmitter and receiver all built into one unit. It's hooked to something we call a 'Texas Bugcatcher' antenna at the right rear bumper. It's a larger version of the shorter one on the roof you've already seen, but for a different type of radio. From this rig, using the big antenna, I can literally talk anywhere in the world, depending on how I set these controls. It requires a federal license which I got when I was a teenager.

"Okayyyy," she said nodding her head.

"I just totally geeked you out, didn't I?"

"Well, no – not really," she said. "I had heard of Ham Radio Operators, but never actually met one. So, you guys like lots of radios and pork?" she asked with a grin.

"Oh yes," he said, "but the former more than the latter. I can do without the pork chops."

That got a small giggle.

"I have a similar, if somewhat larger rig at home – several actually. They're all in one of the rooms you've not been in. I have made friends all over the world, and even used it a couple of times during emergency situations."

"Really? Like what?"

"Well," he began, "there was a really severe tornado that struck a town nearby when I was in high school, and a friend and I took our portable radio gear over there and handled emergency communications in and out of the area for a couple of days. The phone lines were down and we were virtually the only quick communications available. The local officials were pretty glad to see us."

"Really?" she said. "That's amazing. So you saw all the damage up close?"

"Well, kinda. We were set up in a not-so-damaged motel just on the edge of the affected area, but we drove through that area the day we left. It was a real mess. Several people lost their lives. That was not so cool."

"Well, I guess not!" she said. "But at least you were able to help."

"Yeah," he said.   "We thought so. We both received commendations afterwards, and *that* was kind of cool."

"So, can I see it work?"

"Sure!" Tom powered it up, set it up on 20 meters, and turned up the volume. The sound was wired into the car's audio system, so the sound came from all around. Her eyes got big.

Tom tuned around and found a conversation going on near the top of the band.

"....*and we were on Staten Island years ago, so we decided to look up the house where the wedding scene was shot for 'The Godfather', but that thing was on a dead end street and suddenly the whole idea got a little creepy, so we got the heck out of there! W1UBF, W7AFS*"

15

Tom had the mike in his hand so he keyed the 'transmit' button and just said "Whiskey Three Tango Tango".

They waited a few of seconds and Kathy asked, "OK, what happened?"

"Well, we're only hearing one side of the conversation. Because of the way signals are reflected off the earth's ionosphere, we sometimes only hear one of the stations."

"So, what do you do?"

"Just sit here and wait for the other station to pass the conversation back to the first guy," he explained. "I know from the number in his call letters the guy we can hear is probably on the west coast, and that the guy he's talking to is probably in New England."

"So why do we hear the guy who's the farthest away, and not the guy who's closer?"

"That's just how these reflected radio waves work," he said. "The guy who's talking now that we can't hear is actually too far away to be heard directly, and the sky wave he's talking to the first guy on is skipping over us." She screwed up her brow. "I know," he said. "It's seems strange. But welcome to the world of electromagnetic physics!"

Shortly, the first voice came back on.

"*W1UBF, W7AFS returning. I know what you mean, Larry. So much of what's on TV is just as fake as it can be. I think we had a breaker just as I turned it back to you. Whiskey Three Tango Tango, Whiskey Seven Alpha Foxtrot Sierra. You still there, old man?*"

Tom again keyed the mike. "Yes, W7AFS, this is Whiskey Three Tango Tango mobile Four. Name here is Tom, Tango Oscar Mike, and I'm stationary mobile in Arlington Virginia. Just showing

16

the rig to my YL friend Kathy here, so how copy? W7AFS, W3 Tango Tango Mobile."

He released the mike switch and the speakers came back to life.

"W3TT, W7AFS. Good afternoon, Tom, and greetings to your friend Kathy. Name here is Pete, Papa Echo Tango Echo, and you're five-nine plus 10 at my palatial villa located just outside Seattle. OK – it's really just a two bedroom flat, but it's on one of the most scenic lots you can imagine, hi hi. Rig is the Collins S-Line feeding a home-brew tribander up fifty feet. On the other end is Larry just outside Boston. So, how copy? W3TT, W7AFS."

Tom keyed the mike and said, "W7AFS, Whiskey Three Tango Tango, very good, Pete. Your S-Line sounds great. I have one at my home QTH as well. I'm not hearing Larry, but you're a solid five nine plus here as well, and the rig is a Kenwood TS120 feeding the Bugcatcher on the bumper. Kathy and I both work in a government office primarily in transportation," and he gave Kathy a wink! "I don't want to monopolize the conversation, I just wanted to show Kathy how Ham Radio works, so I'll drop out and let you get back to your QSO. Hopefully Kathy's sufficiently impressed with Amateur Radio. So, 73's from a parking lot in Virginia, and maybe I'll catch you later on down the log. W7AFS, Whiskey Three Tango Tango Mobile Four."

"OK, nice to hear you, Tom, and your lovely friend Kathy there. And sure – give us a shout any time we're on. 73's to ya', W3TT, W7AFS, and Larry, that was Tom mobile in Virginia showing off his ham rig to a young lady. Lucky him! Anyway, I was at a meeting the other day at the ....."

Tom turned down the volume and went on to explain all Kathy had just heard.

"The QSO is shorthand for an on-air contact," he told her. "We exchanged some numbers indicating how strong our signals were at each end. The 'Whiskeys' and 'Tangos' were simply phonetic alphabet representations for the letters in my call sign. Whiskey is for 'W', 'Tango' is for 'T', and so forth. As you know, my home, or 'QTH', is just over the state line in Delaware so my callsign has a '3' in it, but since I'm in a vehicle I have to identify as 'mobile', and where we are right now is in the 4th call sign district – hence the 'Mobile Four'. We exchanged our equipment setup, and ended with the '73', which is shorthand for kind-of a handshake-on-the-air. It comes from back in the days when Morse code was used and kept people from having to spell out the entire phrase, just as the 'hi, hi' he mentioned is shorthand for a laugh. Normally we'd get much more involved in a conversation, but I didn't want to break up the one he had going with Larry who, as I said before, we can't hear. Anyway, that's Ham Radio in miniature. There is much much more to the hobby, but the bread and butter is one to one contact between two different individuals. It may be a king to a pauper, or a congressman to a cook. You never know who'll be on the other end."

"How do you know how to get in contact with these other hams," she asked.

"Well," Tom said, "we have certain segments of the radio spectrum that we're allowed by international law to operate in. Over time, you just learn where certain parts of the world might be available and what time of the day. It's also cyclical, in that the earth's ionosphere is charged by particles coming from the sun's sunspots. When there are plenty of sunspots, the ionosphere is highly charged and may reflect signals all day and way into the night. When there aren't many sunspots, not so much. I know, for example, that we're in a moderate part of the sunspot cycle, so if I tune into the spectrum above 10 Megahertz, I can likely bounce my signals off the ionosphere to the other side of the country, or the other side of the world. If I want to talk to people nearer, I tune to the spectrum below 10 Megahertz, where the physics of the signals allow them to more follow the earth's surface for longer distances rather than be bounced off the ionosphere. If you're new to the hobby, there are charts and graphs, as well as those who've been on for a while, all of whom are glad to help."

"Why do you refer you as an 'old man', and to me as a, what was it, 'YL'?" she asked.

"Oh," Tom said, 'Old man' is a term that evolved over the years for another male ham. 'YL' is another abbreviation for 'Young Lady'. We have lots of shorthand terms – maybe too many. Interestingly, when the 'YL' is someone's wife, she's referred to as the 'XYL'. I will always be an 'old man', though"

"Well, I guess that makes sense, in a weird way," she said with a chuckle. "So, you said you have to get a icense to do this? What is involved?"

"Basically a written test. There are several classes of license, some with more privileges than others. I have the highest class of license called the 'Extra' class, and it, of course, has the hardest test. I have to renew my license every few years, but all that requires is a form to be filed with the FCC."

"So, anybody can get a license?" she asked.

"Yep – unless you're a criminal or something. All you have to do is pass the test, and then obey the rules."

"Who enforces the rules? Do they have radio police?" she asked with a chuckle.

"Well, kind of," he said. "The Amateur Radio Service is pretty much self policing. We value the privileges we have enough to make sure those who misbehave are held accountable. Because of how we act and use the spectrum we're assigned, the FCC thinks highly of hams, not to mention the fact that in an emergency we're a ready national communications resource they can depend on. We like to keep that relationship in place."

"Interesting, that sounds like a fun hobby..." she said.

"I think so. Anyway, I enjoy it. OK, so I've sufficiently geeked you out enough. Still wanna be seen with me?"

She smiled warmly. "Oh, yes. Yes I do!"

That earned her a smile and a peck on the cheek. That was the final step in Tom's journey to 'she's the one'. Tom had been to her house a number of times and he was impressed with how well decorated her apartment was, and the meals she prepared were off the charts delicious. The fact that she was great at baking was just the icing on the cake, so to speak. Tom realized he might want to be careful, or his waist line might change in the wrong direction!

Tom had not been necessarily thinking about marriage when he met Kathy, but the more time he spent with her, the more time he wanted to spend with her. Little had he known that the 'I'm not looking to get married' quip he'd made when they first started dating was not at all accurate.

Their dating continued and a few weeks later one Friday night, Tom had been able to get good tickets for a concert. He picked up Kathy and they had a nice few hours together. Later, as he pulled back up at her apartment, and turned off the engine, they sat in silence for a few moments when Tom said, "I love you, you know." She looked over at him with smiling brown eyes and said "I love you, too". He held her hands as they kissed, and from that point on it was just a matter of time.

CHAPTER 4
Pasadena, CA

2001

Lew left Lydia's office and went to his office for a few moments to gather his materials for the morning class. He had scheduled only one today, but he would be done in plenty of time for his lunchtime meeting. In fact, he'd not been sleeping too well lately - his right hip had been giving him problems waking him up frequently during the night - so he figured he might even have time for a short nap before lunch. That was the plan, anyway. These days the office couch seemed to be more comfortable than his bed at home.

This morning's class was for a course that covered civilization from Babylon through the end of the Roman Empire. As such, it was one of Lew's favorite courses to teach and, indeed, he'd been instrumental in bringing it to Caltech, and had actually authored the textbook. An accomplished author, Lew spoke French, Spanish, and had a working knowledge of Russian, which he learned while spending a year in Moscow doing research. He had written several treatises on philosophy and history over the years, and in this morning's class he would be discussing the changes taking place around the time of the Roman Emperors Julius Caesar and Tiberius and the part they played in the establishment of what would eventually become Germany. It was this event, along with others, that Lew was wanting to fully develop with the grant he was hoping to get.

The class was relatively small compared to some other courses, with only about thirty in attendance. As such, it helped make the discussions more lively and the teaching environment more intimate. While he had an ego as would any professor, and lecturing a full auditorium would certainly stoke that ego, in this case he really loved the smaller class. It gave him more latitude in each class session.

"As we have discussed, while everyone agrees that Rome was a significant world power, her influence in world affairs is even more significant than most people concede. But, the reality of the eventual creation of Germany is also much more significant than most historians admit. In fact, you can draw a straight line from these two Roman Emperors, through Germany, straight to the ascendancy of the United States as a world power in the 20th Century," he told the assembled students. "Without the development of the Germanic tribes into what eventually became Germany, and in particular the Battle of Teutoburg Forest in 9 CE, Hitler would never have ascended to threaten the world, the U. S. would have never gone to war in Europe in the 20th Century, and Japan would not have been emboldened to expand its empire so vociferously. As a result, the United States would not have grown into the world power it is today, because we were able to leverage the condition that the rest of the world was war-torn and we were not. Additionally, nuclear weapons would not have been developed, at least in the timeline they were. There would have been no Manhattan Project, because it would not have been necessary without the Axis powers threatening the world. The United Nations would not have developed as it did, and it's entirely possible that England would still be at or near the top of the power chain, rather than being dwarfed by the United States. Without Rome's loss to the Germanic tribes, one can argue that neither of the two World Wars of the 20th Century would have even been fought – the two events that generated massive changes in the power structures of the world. Additionally, without the horrors the Nazis committed in World War Two, there would have been no impetus to re-establish the nation of Israel as a haven for the Jewish people, Thus, the Roman Emperors and the decisions they made were pivotal in the establishment of the U.S. as we know it today. This, and other events, are seminal events in not only world history, but in our own history as well."

"Dr. Donaldson, do you discount the effects of Christianity on our development down through history?" The question came from Katie, a young lady sitting in the front row. She had, for the most part, been a quiet student so far, but Lew always solicited questions from his students - particularly those that challenged generally accepted beliefs, because such questions inevitably resulted in interesting debates.

"Actually, no, I do not," he said, as he sat down on the corner of his desk. "There are a myriad of cultural influences, including the rise of the Christian sects, which had major influences on our development as well. But, as I said earlier, there are certain singularly seminal events one can point to that were crucial for the history of not only our nation, but of the world as a whole. Imagine, for instance, again as I alluded to earlier, if there had been no Germany - if it had simply been another province of the Roman Empire. The historical changes that took place as a result of their existence, beginning in 9 CE, would never have taken place. Rome's greatest defeat led to our becoming a world power."

"I understand that," said Katie, "but aren't Christianity and Judaism more of an influence?"

"More of an *influence*? Arguably. But, what is more of the *cause* of such events? The desire for religious sects to practice their beliefs has always provided an impetus, down through history, for activities such as the migration of religious groups from Europe to the Americas. But, one of the things I intend to establish is just how much of a *root cause* events such as Germany's establishment were, and there is a difference between cause and influence. The fact that these influences occurred along the same time as the Christian Sects were being established is mere coincidence. Without the root cause beginning at Tetuoburg, any resulting influences are inevitably inconsequential," and as he spoke, he closed his book, got up from his desk, and said, "and with that, unfortunately, we'll have to pause until our next session. Read Chapter Ten by next time and we'll see where Tiberius takes us."

The class broke up, and Lew and headed for his office. It was just after 9:00, and it would be a couple of hours before he had to get ready for the meeting, so in his mind he was already napping on the couch in his office.

As the students left the classroom and went their separate ways, Katie unobtrusively lingered in the classroom until it was empty. She then went over to Dr. Donaldson's desk, took something out of her backpack, and placed it in the top right-hand drawer of his desk. She knew he used that drawer to store items he brought with him to the classroom, so she was certain he would notice the book she put there. On the inside cover of the book Katie had placed a typed note that simply said '*For Dr. Donaldson - I thought you might find this interesting. I know I have.*' She had not put her name on it. Having done that, Katie

25

quickly closed the drawer and hurried to her lab class, hoping she wouldn't be late.

Coming down the hallway Lew entered his office, locked his door, and went over to his desk and opened a file on his computer's desktop. It was his personal journal he used to keep his class notes, and he had forced himself to keep detailed notes, especially after a few embarrassing events – one in which he taught the same lesson twice to the same class. So, he went to the end of the journal, entered the date, and made a few notes about what he'd gone over, as well as the comments from some of his students, including the comment by Katie. As he wrote that note he smiled to himself. She was a nice young lady, but she was a Microbiology student, and he had his doubts about her fully understanding the importance of certain historical events. He then checked his email, replied to a couple, then remembered he'd left his all his materials, including the notebook with his travel schedule in it, back in the classroom. He logged off, got up from his desk, and went back down to the classroom to retrieve everything. When he got there, he gathered the materials on top of his desk, then opened the drawer where he'd stored his notebook during class, but he noticed another book with his name on it. Frowning for a moment, he took the book, stared at the title, then opened the cover. On the inside was a note, and as he read it he shook his head. He retrieved his notepad from the drawer, shut it, and took all the items back down to his office and put them on his desk.

When he was assembling his office, his now-estranged wife had given him a couch, knowing how sometimes he got involved in his work and could use it to take a nap. It was a really comfortable couch. On the end table beside the couch, he retrieved an alarm clock he kept there and programmed a wake-up alarm for 11:00, which would give him plenty of time to get fully awake, pack for his trip to the conference, change clothes, drag a brush through his hair, and make the trip over to the restaurant for his meeting with Lydia and the Education Department representatives. He took his pen our of his shirt pocket and his billfold out of his hip pocket and put them on his desk, then put the clock back where it was, making sure the alarm-set light was on. Then he adjusted the pillow and lay down for a short nap. Even though his mind could be swirling with ideas and things he wanted to explore, he had the ability to just turn it off any time he needed a few minutes of quiet. He counted himself lucky to do so. Many of his colleagues had complained they just couldn't turn their minds off when they just needed a few minutes of rest.

He took three deep breaths, relaxing as he did, emptied his mind, and focused on the insides of his eyelids.

CHAPTER 5
Arlington, VA

Early 1980s

Before Tom and his group had started actual development on the project, there were lots of meetings, discussions, position papers, and even a couple of heated arguments among some members, of exactly how to do this. The complexity of the project, and all its components, grew exponentially from what Tom had even initially imagined. This could eventually rival the scope of the Manhattan Project, but only in its effect and the amount of funds required to achieve it, not necessarily in the number of people actually working on it. Tom's idea had always been to actually build the 'Star Trek' transporter using one of two possible methods: (1) Make a scan of the item at the molecular level, then 'print' or 're-assemble' the article, molecule by molecule, at the destination ('replication'), leaving the origin intact and untouched; or (2) actually do a physical transfer from one time/location to another ('transfer') where the original article is actually transported from it's place and time to another place and time! In the TV series, they don't tell you how they do it, but the visual in the series indicated the replication method was used, meaning that a copy was made and "reassembled" at the destination. However, to accomplish this, the original would have to be destroyed to prevent multiple 'copies' of everyone running around.

Tom could be wrong, but that was really the only way to do the way they portrayed it.

To do either method, though, they would have to open a space/time portal – a 'window' between the original and its destination and freeze that window in place until either the replication or the transfer was complete. That meant they would have to learn how to warp the fabric of space and time, actually creating a 'wormhole', the 'portal' through space and time that allowed access to a place where they desired, and more importantly, a *time* they desired. This was very 'science-fiction-y' (a term Tom used to the amusement of those around him), and none of the technology yet existed anywhere but in science fiction, so they would have to design and build it. Tom had made it clear from the beginning that this would be a long and arduous process. Nevertheless, DARPA was in for the long haul.

Their discussions thought through both methods. In Tom's mind both had problems, but in both models they still needed the 'wormhole' to access a location and time in the immediate past. Both methods required determining the exact shape and size of the object to be transferred, which was easy enough for something they could actually 'get their hands on'. A physical transfer would required that 'window' be designed to exactly fit the shape and size of the object to be transferred, then the 'window' would be moved 'through' that object, immediately moving it the object from it's current space and time to the other space and time selected by the portal. It would simply vanish from one time and appear in the other, even though the 'other' might only be five minutes ago a thousand miles away! The 'replication' method also required this size/shape measurement to know where and of what to make a copy.

Although there were valid reasons for doing an actual transfer, Tom considered this a more messy, and perhaps more dangerous solution. Besides, it could not even be tested without this 'portal', while the 'replication' method could be tested by hard-wiring the source and destination devices. Thus, his preference was the replicate method, even though it required the development of both the molecular scanning and printing equipment that did not yet exist. But they could at least begin work on those two devices while waiting on others to figure out the portal that would eventually be necessary. So, Tom decided to flesh out all the possibilities and ramifications by placing all options on the table. In the end, these were only the two: Tom's scan/reassemble idea ('replicate'), or actually physically move the item ('transfer') across the portal. There were, then, the two camps: Those who insisted the physical transfer was the best way, and Tom's camp that insisted the replicate method was right, but their discussions led to valid arguments for both methods, so they would do initial development on both ideas. Tom felt confident that in the end, his method would be the preferred one, but it wouldn't hurt to have both methods available just in case.

The software to accomplish all this would be extremely complex, so Tom put two software development teams in place: The 'transfer' team, and the 'replication' team. Tom had a minor in computer science, so naturally he wanted to keep a watch on both teams' developments. Initially, though, both had to work together, because whichever track they took, there would have to be many ~~some~~ common elements in the software code required to 'cross the Rubicon' of time. There were several problems, not the least of which was that this was all just theoretical. Even if they had the software written and the hardware invented, the key to all this, no matter which option was eventually chosen, was how to actually open a portal in time. The solution to that would eventually turn out to be years in the future (there's that time problem again!) - in Switzerland.

There was a consortium of scientists that wanted to build a very large particle accelerator that some thought *might* have the possibility, among other things, of creating a 'wormhole' in the fabric of space that might, *might*, allow the peering back into time by creating a portal to the past. There had been, for decades, various particle accelerators in existence, and indeed Tom's Master's thesis had dealt with the use of these devices to open a wormhole portal, and that concept was what had attracted the attention of DARPA. However, none of the existing particle accelerators were anywhere near powerful enough to create even the smallest 'wormhole' or 'portal', and even if they did, the ramifications of creating one were unknown. Unbeknownst to Tom when he first discussed his project with DARPA (and, as it turns out, everyone else), DARPA had already been very interested in the possibilities such an 'accelerator' might open up, both scientifically and militarily, so they had convinced the powers-that-be in Washington to, while keeping the source and purpose secret, help fund this development. Funding would always be an ongoing struggle, since Congress had to authorize expenditures on an annual basis, and now Tom's project was so top secret that only a few in government would ever really know of its existence, and no one outside a small circle of scientists would be aware of the details of Tom's project.

To accomplish the necessary funding, DARPA and the National Science Foundation decided that the NSF would be the source on paper, but in reality, DARPA would be providing the lion's share of the funding. When Tom was still in college, his time/space/transfer/copy idea came up in a meeting he and several others attended with a DARPA representative sent to their campus to recruit new talent. That representative instantly connected the dots between Tom's idea and this accelerator project, which is why Tom was recruited and ended up at DARPA in the first place.

While the team could still begin development work on the software, hardware development was also a major component, and since all this would be highly classified, the funding, then, had to be 'hidden' without violating any laws or regulations, and that was no small detail! DARPA, however, had plenty of legal experts and accountant types who were very accomplished at doing that very thing. The problem with all this subterfuge was, though, that funding was allocated on a non-recurring basis, meaning there were plenty of times when the funds from one source had simply run out, and the team had to await funding from another source before continuing.

It was during one of these 'dry' periods that Kathy had come into the picture, and truth be told, she is one reason Tom relinquished most of his responsibilities guiding the software development. He was not going to let her get out of the picture, so he made her a priority at least as high as opening portals in space and time.

Tom's relationship with Kathy was progressing to the point that they were seeing or talking to each other pretty much every day, and they spent most weekends together. Tom even started going to her church. Her pastor, Bro. Moore, was an exceptionally good speaker, and his sermons had a certainty and a definite authenticity to them. Every Sunday morning Tom would go by and pick up Kathy, and they would attend her Sunday School class and worship service, after which they'd spend the rest of the day on afternoon dates that most of the time ended only when they each realized they had to go to work in the morning.

Going to church with her each Sunday caused Tom to take a good long look at his own life. Seeing Kathy's faith, and liking what he saw, put many of his own decisions in perspective. Tom had accomplished much as a physicist, and his personal life was doing pretty well, but there still seemed to be something missing. Just what was the point? If they were able to do all this, so what? He had a couple of long discussions with Kathy about her beliefs, and she introduced him to many parts of the Bible he had not really paid much attention to, even though his parents had taken him to church since his childhood. Tom realized one Sunday morning though that if, in the end, all he had was his name on a scientific development, no matter how huge it was, he was still going to end up being not much more than that pile of dirt they were using for raw material. In the end, it was the sermon one Sunday morning where Bro. Moore asked that very question: *'If you died today, what would your life amount to?'* Tom simmered on that one all week long. The answer was, *'not much'*. He wanted his life to matter more than that. Finally, those words came back to him as the pastor read, in one of his sermons, Matthew 16:26. *'What will it profit a man if he gains the whole world, but loses his soul?'* Yeah – what about that?

The following Sunday morning, Tom slipped out of his seat next to Kathy and walked down the isle to where the Bro. Moore was waiting. As he approached, a warm smile grew on the pastor's face. He knew. Tom told him he wanted that free gift Christ had promised, and wanted to follow Him, and actually make something out of his life. From that point on, Tom began to prepare for a life beyond. It turns out he mattered to Someone who had cared enough to pay his entry fee into what He had told the thief on the cross was 'paradise'. Kathy was elated, as were Tom's parents whom he called as soon as he got back to his apartment. He hadn't known until that day how much they'd all been praying for him. The pastor's sermons on the crucifixion and the reality of who Christ was had a certainty to them, and Tom didn't realize just how certain that really was until he met the Messiah down at the altar that day. As he left the church that morning, Tom took one look back at the Cross that hung in the baptistery and in his mind's eye imagined the sacrifice that was paid on his account. He remembered the words Christ had said to the Apostle Thomas that day, '*Thomas, you have seen Me. But blessed are they who have not seen, and yet they believe.*'

In the meantime, the funding situation had given Tom more time to spend with Kathy. That gave them both plenty of time to talk about all sorts of things, and one of the things was their relationship. Tom was ready for the next step.

He believed she was as well.

Every year Tom took part in something called "Field Day", where local Ham Radio Operators would set up portable stations outdoors off the grid to simulate emergency operations. It doubled as a national on-the-air contest with other similar stations across the country, and it was a huge event in the Ham Radio world. Tom had not missed one since he became licensed as a teenager. This year, however, he had something else on his mind, and it suddenly was more important than a playing 'emergency' on radios in a field somewhere.

He picked up Kathy at home and they spent the afternoon together. First, they went to a small theater to watch a movie - they were playing '*Raiders of the Lost Ark*'. They had both already seen it, but when he brought up seeing it, she insisted she really liked it, so off they went to see it again. Afterwards they took the thoroughfare headed out of town, and as they drove they just enjoyed the time talking and spending time together. Tom had a friend who had a retreat at nearby Lake Barcroft. His property included a dock on the lake, and he'd offered the use of his boat for today. Tom had promised Kathy they would have a meal out on the water as they watched the sun go down, and then they'd come back to the dock and go home before darkness fully set in. She thought it was just a nice evening on the water. Well, it was, but there was something else.

Just as the sun was touching the horizon, Tom kissed her, and while he was doing that he reached in his pocket, pulled out a small case, and when they finished the kiss he held it up between them. Her eyes grew wide as she realized what it was, her mouth flew open, and Tom asked her to marry him.

Needless to say, getting a "YES! YES!" from his now-fiance was a major highlight of Tom's life. They didn't make it back to the dock before dark. Neither wanted the day to end. They talked into the evening about what their lives might be like, when to have the wedding, where to live, what about kids, where to get married - all questions that had to be answered. Asking them gave them time to dream together.

They would soon decide to have the wedding in the early summer, probably June, and Kathy wanted to have the wedding at their church. Tom had joined her church at the same time he had accepted Christ as his Savior.

The weekend had gone by way too fast though, and come Monday everyone at work knew something was up. When Tom told them he and Kathy were engaged, it was not a real shock to anyone.

"I knew you guys would get there," Leonard deadpanned. "It was obvious to everyone. We knew you had lost your first love."

"What do you mean?" Tom asked.

"Physics will now be a read-headed stepchild, Tom. But, that's not a bad thing. Maybe it'll help you understand when the rest of us complain about getting hooked."

"Hey!" said one of the ladies in the back. Everyone laughed.

"Well, if this is what 'hooked' feels like, I wish I'd bitten sooner. Anyway, today we have work to do."

"Yeah, I knew the break wouldn't last long," said Leonard with a mock groan.

"OK!" Tom said. "Nose. Grindstone. Make it happen!" and clapped his hands to more mock groans all around the room.

During all this, the tweaking and testing, coupled with the inevitable delays in funding, Tom and Kathy spent a lot of time together. She bought her wedding dress and Tom bought the rings. His was, of course, the standard man's gold ring. Hers was a beautiful clustered ring that was a match to the engagement ring he'd given her. They set the wedding for the first Friday in June, and sent out the invitations. Tom took her to Mississippi to meet his parents one weekend – a very successful outing. Kathy and Tom's mother became instant friends and Tom's Dad told him he was shocked Tom had convinced anyone of Kathy's beauty and intelligence to spend more than a day with him. "Thanks a lot, Dad!" Tom had said.

The following weekend the couple went to Texas and met her family. That weekend went well, and they decided to set another date for both families to get together in 'neutral' territory. They chose Hot Springs, Arkansas, and Tom made the reservations. Three weeks later Tom and Kathy took a couple of personal days, which worked out well since there was still a 'hole' in the funding schedule, so they spent a long weekend in Arkansas with both families where everyone bonded and decided they might just do this on a semi-regular basis. Tom's Dad and Kathy's brother developed a bond, and Kathy's Mom and Tom's Mom became friends and would keep in touch with each other long after they'd all quit making these treks to Arkansas.

As the DARPA project grew, it got to the point that Tom really needed a good office administrator and someone to help him keep track of everything. It turned out he had the perfect candidate! He asked Kathy if she wanted the job and she jumped at it. Ted hated to give her up, but he was a stand-up guy, and totally understood. Besides, his project was beginning to wind down. Talk about Providence! So, one Monday morning, Tom no longer had to run into Kathy in the hallway. She was in the adjacent office. Tom and Kathy turned out to be a dynamic duo, and she fit really well into the group. Everything seemed to be lining up!

Six months later, Tom and Kathy stood in her home Church before Bro. Moore and said their vows while their families and close friends looked on, both sets of parents full of proud smiles. When they returned from the honeymoon to Nantucket, they consolidated their personal belongings into a new home they'd purchased not far from where they worked. They both wanted children, so Tom and Kathy began their new life together, and Tom thought his project at DARPA would eventually take somewhat of a back seat.

CHAPTER 6
Arlington, VA

Late 1980s

Finally, the Team's renewed funding coincided with the Particle Accelerator development, and the *Conseil Européen pour la Recherche Nucléaire* research facility (better known as CERN) in Geneva, Switzerland, was the lead agency to develop and manage the Accelerator project. When Tom had come on board at DARPA, he was told of the plans to build the Large Electron-Positron Collider (called the 'LEP' for short) on the border of Switzerland and France and the long term plans and the possibilities of future technologies. That's when all the dots got connected in Tom's head, just like those who had recruited him.

But while that was key, it was just part of the problem, and at the time he came aboard at DARPA, it was still very much in the future. Over the length of the project, the LEP would eventually be dismantled and the much larger and much more capable 'Large Hadron Collider' (LHC, also known as the "supercollider") constructed using portions of the tunnels the LEP had utilized. But, before that even became something on their radar, if they were going to use his 'replication' method, the team would need the ability to scan and reassemble anything across some future-possible portal in space/time, so it was a good thing the accelerator was in the future, because they had other fish to fry. They needed a scanner and, oh yes, a printer, both of which worked at the molecular level - neither of which existed!

Fortunately, the wizards in the DARPA labs were already working on a classified project to develop a scanning device to scan physical items at the molecular level and store the result as data. If they were going to use that, though, they would also need a way to re-create an item also at the molecular level. They needed a molecular 'printer', or re-assembler, to recreate the object from the data they'd scanned. DARPA management took the preliminary work done on the scanner and, after several meetings on the subject and how to accomplish it, decided to created another team to reverse the process, and they attached both teams to Tom's program.

There was one problem that ended up having a simple solution. To recreate something on the other side, you can't just make it out of nothing. The Law of Conservation of Matter is very explicit on that point. However, using the example from the Bible in Genesis Chapter 2 where God created man from '*the dust of the ground*', Tom had realized that God had already done this, except, of course, His molecular printer was much more capable! So, by using just an ordinary pile of dirt as the raw material, Tom reasoned they should be able to reorganize it at the molecular level to an exact reproduction of the scanned object. As it turned out, dirt was available everywhere. But, since the Almighty probably wouldn't lend DARPA His 'printer', they had to build their own, including the software to accomplish all this. So, work on all these interconnected projects commenced, with Tom in the middle trying to keep all the balls up in the air.

The programmers who worked on the project were very talented, and since Tom considered himself an above average programmer, he could see just how good these guys really were. This was a vastly complex software system involving hundreds of software programs and literally thousands of subroutines. Many times there were problems or issues to be resolved, and the solutions this team came up with were both innovative and elegant. Tom was working with actual geniuses. The amount and size of the software code grew exponentially. Nights, and weekends were consumed by the teams' members on the unique pieces of the software program.

They were using the 'object oriented' method for creating the software. The entire project was broken down into smaller 'chunks', each of which only performed a specific function. For example, imagine a laundry room that contains a washer, a dryer, and an iron. The 'washer' doesn't know or care what goes on in the 'dryer', it's function is to wash. Likewise, the 'dryer' doesn't know or care how the clothes are cleaned, it's goal is to remove moisture from the items placed in it. Finally, the 'iron' doesn't know or care about washing or drying, all it wants to do is remove wrinkles. By breaking up each function and developing the other functions separately, security could also be maintained, and at one point there were dozens of teams across DARPA working on one of these 'self-contained' functions.

Each of these individual 'functions' had a team of programmers assigned it's task, and many tasks would be identical for both replication and transfer. Sometimes a 'team' was one programmer, and some programmers might work on more than one team. Each team would be given the parameters they needed to work with, and the desired outcome of their particular function, without necessarily having knowledge of the ultimate goal. One of Tom's tasks was to be able to keep up with all the functions and the IT staffs working on them, while at the same time maintaining the ability to keep the proverbial wool from being pulled over *his* eyes, as well as many times keeping the ultimate goal classified. So, as much as he could, Tom reviewed the code from each programming group as it was created and, over time, he felt he had a pretty fair handle on how the software work was progressing. Each different software function's task had a lead programmer that was 'read in' to all or part of the main project, and these section leaders would meet regularly along with Tom to address common problems. Eventually, though, Tom had to put one of the lead programmers in charge of the entire software development, to free the time he needed to manage the teams working on the scanner and printer hardware, but he still kept abreast on how it was all progressing. This was all still very early on, and they had no idea how many weeks, months, and eventually years it would take to make even one of these methods possible.

Their first breakthrough came with the scanning group. The prototype machine they came up with looked like it was made of duct tape and paper clips, but eventually it was ready for a test run. After many fits, starts, and even sometimes emergency runs down to Radio Shack to pick up a resistor, transistor, or just a spool of wire, they were eventually able to get a rudimentary molecular scanner working to the point they could scan a number 2 pencil and store its molecular data in computer memory. That was huge, and took some doing. When everyone was sure they had it working as best they could, Tom took that number 2 pencil, chipped a piece off the eraser, and put his own teeth marks in the side of it. Then they scanned it, stored the data, and Tom put the pencil in a sealed pouch in his office safe so they could eventually compare it to a duplicate. Hopefully, half the problem was solved, at least at a rudimentary level.

Now, they needed to reproduce that data using a molecular re-assembler, essentially a molecular 'printer', so they could reproduce exactly that pencil. This whole process really boiled down to more or less alchemy – what pseudo-chemists had tried all down through history to accomplish and failed. But, then, they didn't have supercomputers.

After years of development they finally accomplished the seemingly impossible. Like the scanner project, they were finally able to try to recreate the scanned pencil. Each time they ran the 'printing' process, the process took nearly two days. But after several attempts, one day when the process ended they opened the door protecting the reassembly chamber, and there sat a number 2 yellow pencil with teeth marks and a piece of the eraser missing. Tom couldn't believe his eyes, so he literally ran to the safe, retrieved the original, and compared it to the duplicate. There it was – an exact copy with the missing chunk out of the eraser he'd made, as well as his own teeth marks on the side! Then he took the *duplicate* over to the scanner and had *it's* structure scanned and turned into data. When he compared the two scanned data sets, they were identical. They had done it! He locked them both in individually sealed pouches in his safe as historical firsts (being careful to label which was the original, and which was the duplicate)! Now it was time to turn their development units into units that could actually be made operational, and that took yet another long period of time to do that development.

With the ability to scan and recreate an item, they got back to the decision of transfer or replicate. By the time they had the scan/print ability, CERN was putting the finishing touches on the Large Hadron Collider, or LHC. That meant, that theoretically and, hopefully soon, they would be able to open that window in space and time. So just what were they going to do with it?

42

Tom and his team continued their work on the project. Kathy became an integral part of the project, and progress, though slow, was occurring. Eventually they settled into a regular routine. One weekend about two years into their marriage, Kathy had insisted they spend the day back on the boat where Tom had proposed. Tom thought this was a great idea, so there they were, in the middle of the lake again. They had just finished a nice meal out on the deck of the boat when Kathy rose and moved her chair next to Tom. She took his hand, kissed him, and presented him with a small square box, just like Tom had when he proposed. A bit surprised, Tom looked into the smiling eyes of his bride, as he opened the box. Inside was an infant's pacifier! Tom's smile changed into a puzzled expression for just a moment, and then wide-eyed elation as the message set in. Seven months later, their first daughter, Kelly, was born, and Kathy took a sabbatical. She stayed home, contributing when she could while she spent those first crucial weeks with her new child. She eventually returned to work, their daughter well attended to in the daycare facility at their church.

While she was an integral part of the team, the progress was slow as they literally invented new technologies, writing and re-writing the software to fit each new parameter. Two years later, Tom and Kathy welcomed a second daughter, whom they named Katie, and made the decision to raise their children as their parents had. One parent would be home for their girls, while the other worked to support their family. As it turns out, their family was as traditional as their parents. Tom worked outside the home, and Kathy worked inside the home – both resolving not to lose focus on their relationships with each other and with their girls. Even though Kathy was now a full-time Mom, she was never out of the loop on the progress at DARPA. When the girls both started school, Kathy worked on a flexible schedule as Tom's Administrative Assistant, and since the school was operated by their Church, which also operated a daycare, she (and sometimes Tom) weren't bound by a strict pick-up schedule when school was out. The girls could stay as late as 5:00 p.m. on days when there was a lot going on at the office, but most days Kathy was there at 3:00 p.m. to pick the girls up and on their way home catch up on their day. Most days Tom was home shortly after 5:00, but again, if something critical was going on, it might be later. On many occasions they would both pick up the girls at school. Life was good.

One evening Tom was in his home 'radio shack' talking to someone on his Ham Radio. Kathy had watched and listened several times, and as she came into the room, she instantly recognized the voice on the other end of the conversation.

"...and we wrapped up just before the evening meal," the voice on the radio was saying, "so I guess I am finished for the week. The weather has been excellent, so I am thankful for that. But, until Monday comes, I have a relaxing weekend planned. So, that's the story this week. I always enjoy our conversations, Tom, and I hope the propagation holds up for the weekend. Maybe we can chat again before the new week. So 73's and Shalom from Jerusalem. K3TT, Four X-ray Four Bravo Sierra."

Tom smiled at Kathy, and pressed the transmit button on his microphone.

"OK, Dan, thanks for the nice QSO. Yeah, I hope the bands hold up this weekend as well, so maybe we can get back together before the weekend's out. Peace to you as well, my brother, and 73's from no man's land near Washington, DC. 4X4BS, Kilo Three Tango Tango off and QRT."

"You and Dan weren't on long this time," said Kathy. "What's going on in Israel tonight?"

"Well," Tom answered, "Dan had a long week, and he was pretty tuckered out. I think he just wanted to get the weekend started. He's a really nice guy, and though he's Hebrew through and through, he still enjoys putting up with us 'Little Christs', as he calls us."

They both chuckled at the original name that eventually became the word 'Christian'.

"Dinner's almost ready," she said. "Come in when you're done while I gather the girls up."

Tom logged the contact in his logbook, shut down his radio gear, and turned off the light as he left the room. When he came into the dining room, Tom noticed something on his plate. It was a small envelope that read '*Open me first*'. When he opened it up, inside was a brand new Amateur Radio License issued to Kathy Reed! As it turns out, Kathy had spent hours studying for her Amateur exam, and had passed the three exams, each more daunting that the last, that garnered her the Extra Class Amateur Radio License NA3TT. In one sitting she had passed all the requirements for the highest class license. When he looked up, she was in the doorway watching him, and when she saw the look on his face, she just giggled.

"When did you do all this?" he asked.

"Well," she said, "what else was I going to do while you were at work and the girls were at school? Besides, I might want to talk to Maddie sometime by myself!"

Maddie was Dan's wife, and they had spoken several times when Tom and Dan would let them. Maddie had her Ham license, but since Kathy didn't, FCC rules only allowed her to talk on the air when Tom was in control of the contact.

Tom jumped up, went over to Kathy and gave her a big hug.

"I'm so proud of you, dear. You really pulled this one over on me. I had no idea!" he said. "AND, you even co-opted my callsign. What a surprise!"

"That was kind of the goal," she said, "that you would have no idea. Looks like I pulled it off."

"I wish you'd told me before I signed off with Dan," Tom said. "He could have set something up between you and Maddie."

"Oh, I have that one figured out," she said. "The next time you get on the air with Dan, I'll 'break in' to your conversation and ask if Maddie's home, then tell them both."

Tom laughed. "That'll do the trick!"

Just then their eldest daughter came in the room.

"What trick?" she asked.

Kathy answered, "Oh, that thing I told you about this afternoon. I just told your Dad."

"Oh great," she said with a smirk. "Another one. Are you guys going to build another room for your 'gear'?"

Tom and Kathy looked at each other and fell out laughing.

"I don't think it's so funny", Kelly said as she sat down at the table. That caused them to laugh even harder, and they both hugged her as they all sat down to eat.

CHAPTER 7
Arlington, VA

Late 1990s

While the replication team was working on the scan/print projects, the transfer team also made progress on the software for their assignment. Their idea was to open a portal adjacent to the object to be moved, then actually move the portal 'through' the object, immediately moving it to the other side of the portal, or the other 'time'. One second you're in New York at 8:25 a.m. local time, and the next you're seven timezones away in Baghdad at 1:15 p.m. local time. The transfer would be instantaneous. The parameters involved had to be exact. Foul up one variable in the process and you could do some real damage, on a scale which might be hard for the average person to imagine. The key to all of this was the software, so it had to work perfectly! The team had actually discussed the side bets engineers on the Manhattan Project had with each other before the first atom bomb was detonated. The outcomes they had bet on ranged from nothing, to the complete destruction of earth.

The same risk was true on the scan/re-assemble side of the equation, but the prevailing wisdom was that this process was less likely to cause the kind of damage that an actual transfer would if something went wrong. Tom was committed to do no damage, other than, of course, what the guys in uniforms might need to do. So, the first thing he had the group do, after getting the scanner and re-assembler working, was to move these two critical devices to a secure facility in the New Mexico desert just in case, which left their offices looking less high-tech. But safety first, right? Anyway, the hardware didn't have to be anywhere special, since space/time portals could be 'opened up' anywhere at any time adjacent to any and all necessary locations on the planet and do their work. Open up a portal between the item to be scanned and the scanner, scan in the item to be replicated, and open a new portal to the destination. Then 'print' the object on the other side of the portal and presto-changeo, item duplicated. There was an immense amount of code involved in both methods, and it was extremely complex, but the coding team felt like they'd done their very best to eliminate errors.

One thing you have to know about software, though: It doesn't take much of anything for an error to occur. Everyone that has a computer system has, at some point, experienced the infamous 'blue screen of death', but that was something that they simply couldn't afford. If there were any mistakes, they had to be small.

In the grand scheme of things, the mistake that eventually *did* happen actually was small.

But only in the grand scheme of things.....

CHAPTER 8
Arlington, VA

Mid 2000s

The team had already been successful in scanning and replicating inanimate objects, but now they were working on methods of replicating biological entities, and there were problems. Since living beings are never really still (the blood is always flowing, the heart is always beating, the brain is always working), they had figured out a way to 'freeze' something biological in time, scan it at the molecular level, then re-open another window in time and reverse the process, creating a duplicate - at least that was the idea. But, unlike testing of inanimate objects, testing of biologics actually required a portal in which they could "freeze" time, and while both methods were highly classified, adding the portal aspect of the project was even more so. As such, the folks at the LHC and CERN could never watch what was being done when the team accessed the system, so CERN wasn't allowed to see the running processes. In reality, the LHC's only function was to create the portal between the origin and destination of the items to be replicated or transferred, so only that part of the process had to be hidden. The U.S. government had made the need for absolute secrecy abundantly clear to them at the highest levels, so eventually, for the most part, they understood. But periodically there was a bit of a rub there, particularly when something went wrong.

Unfortunately, Tom was responsible for the biggest 'rub' of all. One simple variable in the software was incorrect, causing them to exceed the parameters set by CERN, and the result included damage to the magnetic structure of the LHC and the leaking of six tons of the liquid helium coolant. To say that CERN was not happy was an understatement of colossal proportions! It took significant considerations, both financial and diplomatic, from the U.S. government to get Tom and his team back in the good graces with the scientists and technicians there, but the financial part of the equation had helped a lot, especially when a U.S. Senator personally delivered the funds and treated the entire CERN crew to a night out at a fancy restaurant. Tom was taken to the 'woodshed' and told, in no uncertain terms, to not let it happen again. He was just glad they didn't cancel their project. CERN manufactured a reason for the shutdown and the resulting necessary repairs. Even though it had actually pointed out a flaw in the LHC, and was entirely paid for, the folks at CERN still had some trepidation in letting the proverbial fox that crashed the LHC back in the hen-house, but Tom's team worked diligently to get re-certified to gain access.

In the development stage of the software, they were unable to 'bum the code', a term used by some of the first hackers to re-process the code where instructions are either eliminated or rewritten more concisely to enable a program to run more efficiently and rapidly. That would come once they had something they could present, and could then go into the 'refinement' process. Right now, there were tens of thousands of 'snippets' of code in the program that needed to be examined before they had the finished product. In the meantime, though, they were just trying to get it to work. Leonard Cavanaugh, the chief of software development for the project, had teams go over the hundreds of thousands of lines of code that monitored parameters all along the way and inserted program 'breaks', or places in the software where if something didn't fall within the norms, the program would just stop and make sure the LHC was safe. The program would then branch to a section in the software that would report where in the program the error had occurred, and display as much information as was possible to allow them to figure out what had happened. They spent untold hours running and rerunning the software through all its paces, eventually culminating in the actual opening and closing of a portal out in the desert adjacent to where the scanner and printer had been relocated! Eventually, the team felt ready to actually try it live.

CHAPTER 9
DARPA - Arlington, VA

Mid 2000s

The project Tom and his team were working on was so secret that they couldn't tell anyone at CERN what they were doing or why it was being done. It was also highly classified at DARPA, and only a handful of people outside the working group even knew the project existed. So, when Tom received a call from Dr. Stevens, his superior in the Project Office, ordering him to accompany him to a briefing at the CIA, he was more than a little disturbed.

They arrived at Langley and after being identified, they were ushered into what turned out to be a highly secure conference area where a bespectacled balding man was waiting.

"Good afternoon, gentlemen. My name is Browning," he said. "Please have a seat", and he motioned to the chairs opposite him at the conference table. Tom and Dr. Stevens both noticed, as they sat down, that there were some documents and a small box on the table in front of Browning.

Mr. Browning passed them both one of the documents, and asked them to review it before continuing. Tom read the document, that basically indicated Mr. Browning had been read in on his project at DARPA, up to and including the latest progress reports he had filed with his supervisor sitting beside him!

"I am fully read-into your project," he said when they'd finished. Then he slid another document to each of them.

"This is a non-disclosure," he continued, "covering any and all details of this meeting. As you can each see, I have already signed it, but I require your signatures before we can begin any discussion."

Tom and his superior each read the document, then after glancing at each other with raised eyebrows and a sideways nod and a shrug of shoulders, both signed their copy. Browning then provided Dr. Stevens with another copy he'd signed.

"This one is for your files," he explained. "Nothing we discuss here may be disclosed to anyone outside this room without written authorization. You may not even disclose who you talked to while you were here, or that we even had this discussion. For all intents and purposes this meeting never happened. Do you have any questions?"

Dr. Stevens glanced again over at Tom, then said, "I have to say this is all a bit ominous. We understand non-disclosures, but what is the purpose of this meeting?"

"The first thing I need to know," he began, "is if there are any developments not disclosed in the progress reports that you, Mr. Reed, have filed with Dr. Stevens, anyone else at DARPA, or anyone else in or outside the government."

Tom was now more nervous than he was when he first entered the room.

"Of course not!" Tom exclaimed. "I have fully disclosed not only the progress, but the lack of progress, and every step we've taken since the project began."

"What about you, Dr. Stevens?" he asked.

"I have the same reply," Dr. Stevens said. "I am fully aware of the status of every project under my direction, including and especially this one. What is your reason for asking? Why are we even here discussing this with the CIA? We've had no inkling that our project was even known outside our own limited group, and very few individuals outside DARPA."

Mr. Browning simply maintained firm eye contact for an uncomfortable moment or two, then without breaking eye contact, put on a latex glove, opened the box, and retrieved something from it and laid it on the table.

"Then perhaps you can help us understand something," he said in an ominous voice.

Tom and Dr. Stevens looked down at the object. It was a very dingy coin with a considerable amount of dirt and tarnish, but it was still recognizable as a U.S. Quarter. They both looked at each other, then back at Mr. Browning.

"This is a U.S. quarter minted in 1998," he explained. "I received a call from a contact in the U.S. Mint earlier this month. He had received this from a contact in the State Department, who had received it from an archaeologist involved in an excavation in Israel."

Without touching the coin itself, both Tom and Dr. Stevens leaned in and examined the quarter. While it was in bad shape, it was definitely a U.S. quarter, and you could still make out the serrated edges, and a bit of the image of George Washington.

"OK," said Tom as he sat back. "It's a quarter, and it's in rough shape, but what does that have to do with us?"

Mr. Browning picked up the coin with his gloved hand, holding it by its edges, and sat back in his chair.

"This coin was found in a space in an excavated wall with other coins consistent with those used during the Roman Empire."

Tom glanced over at Dr. Stevens, and he had the same quizzical look Tom was sure he had on his own face.

"So?" asked Dr. Stevens.

"Their first thought was that someone had corrupted the site, or was trying to pull a fast one on them. So they had it tested. The results prompted them to send the coin to the Denver Mint, where further testing was performed."

He turned the coin over, and there was a small blank spot on the back of the coin they had obviously used as a testing area on the base metal of the coin itself.

"What they discovered," Browning explained, "resulted in many questions that have made their way through the chain of evidence I just described, all the way into this room, and the reason we're asking about your progress."

Then he dropped the bomb.

"Scientific tests all prove conclusively two things: First, this is an actual U.S. quarter minted in 1998 in Denver. Second, all the dating methods for both the sediment *and* the quarter we have available indicate conclusively this particular quarter is at least fifteen-hundred years old."

Then with raised eyebrows and an even more ominous voice, he asked, "So, I must ask, what have you people been up to?"

CHAPTER 10
Pasadena, CA

2001

Katie made it to her lab class just in time for the assignments to be handed out. Her task today was a Gram Staining procedure, something she had done before, but she still had to go through all the steps. She went to the supply room and grabbed some clean slides and the other materials, and started up the Bunsen burner. The Crystal Violet and other solutions had already been placed at her work station, so she carefully began preparing the slide. In a few minutes, after the slide had dried, she placed it under the microscope and, after viewing the results, Katie carefully prepared her report, filed it in the assignment tray the instructor had placed at the front of the room, then went to clean up her work station.

Noticing she was done a bit early, the class instructor, standing in the office door at the front of the lab, motioned for her to come over to her.

"Katie, do you see those containers on the shelf above the rear work station?"

"Yes," said Katie.

"Those have long been due to be cycled out since they've been here forever. We have fresh supplies coming in tomorrow, so would you do me a favor and carefully take those to the disposal room down the hall? There's a rolling table you can use over in the corner."

"Sure!" said Katie, and she went over to the corner, retrieved the rolling table, and moved it adjacent to the rear workstation.

As she did, she noticed the jars looked rather old. They were all less than a quarter full so they wouldn't be very heavy, but she wanted to move them carefully anyway. The jars were about chest high, so she reached up and took the first one and moved it to the rolling table. Then she reached up for the second one. As she was moving it off the shelf, the bottom of the jar ever so lightly touched the corner of the shelf they were sitting on. Ordinarily such a small touch would be inconsequential, but these containers had been there for years and, unknown to Katie, had lost some of their structural integrity. The light touch caused the bottom of the container to fracture in such a way that the entire contents poured through the bottom, and spilled on Katie's pants. Immediately Katie smelled burning fabric and felt a burning sensation in her legs. She screamed, and everyone in the lab froze for an instant. Seeing what had happened, one of the students ran over to the wall by the door where a small red box with a glass front was mounted. She grabbed the small hammer dangling on a chain beside the box, shattered the glass, then slammed the handle of the hammer on the large read button inside the box, then yelled "Chemical Spill!!!" The button triggered a loud klaxon throughout the building that sent everyone else in the facility to scramble towards the exit.

Katie ran towards the door and was met by two other female students who grabbed her under her shoulders and all but carried her down the hall to the showers, where they stripped off her clothing, pushed her under an emergency shower, and hit the 'Emergency Wash' button, which began an immediate deluge of water. The three girls all grabbed nearby towels, soaked them in the water stream, and proceeded to completely wash Katie from head to foot, as well as make sure they had not themselves been contaminated.

Finally, the instructor, clothed now in a large protective apron, came running in with a large robe that she placed on Katie.

"How are you?" she asked. "Are your legs burned?"

Embarrassed, looking down, then back up, Katie answered, "No – I think we got it all in time, But.....what am I going to wear out of here?"

"This robe," said the instructor. "You're going straight to the infirmary. We need to make sure everything's OK."

"I....I'm so sorry.." said Katie. "That thing just fell apart!"

"Don't worry about it," said the instructor. "They probably should have been out of here months ago."

As she left the building, the klaxon still going strong, the ambulance from the infirmary was waiting out front surrounded by all the other students that had exited the building when the alarm went off. It was bad enough everyone was standing around, but at least Katie didn't have to walk all the way to the student parking lot in that big white robe. As the ambulance pulled out of the parking lot, someone finally turned the klaxon off.

An hour later, her roommate came by the infirmary with a change of clothing. Coming into the examination room, it was quickly apparent Katie was fine.

"Thanks for the clothes," Katie said.

"No problem," said her roommate. Then she lowered her head and giggled a bit.

"What's so funny?" Katie asked.

"Everyone's asking who the chemical terrorist is. Ohhhh, you're gonna be famous!"

Katie just put her head in her hands.

CHAPTER 11
Arlington, VA

Mid 2000s

In the days since the last try, Leonard had worked on the software some to try to tighten up the code on the translation portion of the program. This was the part that actually took the parameters sent to it – location, size, destination, etc. - and transformed the molecules from one time window to another, basically making an exact duplicate of one organism to the other window. Since there was plenty of time before the next opportunity opened up at CERN, Leonard had diligently worked on the code, and the rest of the crew were just in maintenance mode, updating system logs, performing maintenance on what equipment they did have, etc. You know – basically marking time.

Tom came in one Friday morning to find Leonard watching an online video, so he decided to needle him a bit. "So, software's fixed? Everything's ready to go?"

"Yeah," he said. "I found the problem from last time. It had branched to the wrong translation code copied from an earlier version. I'm just waiting until we can try it again to see what does and doesn't work. Any hope of getting an earlier window?"

"Nope. I tried to call in some favors, but we pretty much ate them all up when we crashed the LHC. They're just not in the mood. I'm afraid if I keep bugging them we'll be bumped again. But, I may have helped us out some."

Leonard gave Tom a cynical look. "What did you do?" he deadpanned.

"Well, I got Kathy to help me out. She got me in touch with some of her family in Texas, and we sent a side of their best beef from their ranch over to Switzerland! I told them to have a party on us."

Leonard's mouth flew open. "How did you figure that out?"

"Well, I was talking….OK, begging….one of the guys over there and he mentioned that he'd been to the States a few years back and really loved the steaks at one of the restaurants he'd been to, so I told him '*well, the best beef in the world comes from Texas – how 'bout I send you some?*' and he bit. So, one thing led to another and next thing you know I have a full side of beef packaged in dry ice headed to Switzerland."

Leonard was incredulous. "That must have cost a pretty penny!"

"Well, the shipping was tough, but Kathy got me the beef at a really good price, and even had her family down there pack it up and ship it for me. Not only that, they sent me a sample. It's good stuff!"

"That's great, man!" he said with a big smile. "You guys look good together, too. Just don't do something stupid."

"Never!" Tom said in mock offense. "So, what do we need to do to be ready for the next window?"

"Can you speed up time?"

"No, but get me on the LHC and I can slow it down," he laughed.

Finally the day came. While both teams (replication and transfer) of designers felt assured their portion of the software was ready for testing, Tom decided to use the replication method for testing. If that worked, then they would know the paramaters for "finding" an object was working, and they could then simply choose the transfer part of the software rather than the replicate part of the software and a physical transfer would hopefully be accomplished. But, safety first!

Kathy's role in the project had grown, not because she had married her boss, but her intelligence and work ethic had fully assimilated her into the group, plus she really wanted to see this part work. So, she was on hand for the desert test where the tents were located, but initially Tom would not let her actually inside the tents – he assigned someone else to monitor the goings on in the tents, at least for the first two-way test. Maybe he was a bit overprotective, but in the event something weird did happen, Tom certainly didn't want anything to happen to his wife! So, he put her in charge of communications. He thought she'd be safe handling the handie-talkie – besides, she had been a licensed Ham since late 80s! The guys in the project, though, let him know about his apparent disregard for them, but it was mostly in jest. Well.....mostly.

The entire operation to be performed, a complete scan and reassembly, an exact copy – atom-by-atom, of an item from one location to another location – was ready for the test. It was the pencil again. It worked perfectly! So, they now knew they could duplicate an inanimate object. It was then time to duplicate something living – a 'biologic'. Freezing the 'window' at a specific time and place, making the scan, then replicating the biologic from one location to another location, would take a while, but since they were 'freezing' time, time would, essentially stand still during

61

the scan process, and again during the reassembly process, only being released once the reassembly was completed.

They had toyed with the idea of actually copying a human from one point to another through these frozen time windows, but in the end, cooler heads had prevailed, and they had made the decision to not actually risk human life in the process. The worst that could happen would be a bad copy which could then just be destroyed without affecting the original in any way. That's a really nice way of saying this could really get messy on the receiving end if things didn't go right.

So, this time, by creating a wormhole from the molecular scanner to the object, located in a tent in the desert near where the scanner and re-assembler were located, then freezing the window, copying the contents therein, they could get a good copy. At the same time, they would open another wormhole in a similar tent located some one hundred feet away, freeze that window in place, then reproduce the copy made by the first one.

The subject was a cockroach sitting in a translucent container dangling from a string in the first tent. A portal would open, a copy made of the cockroach, then recreated through another portal in the second tent into another identical container dangling from a string there. Then DNA samples of both would verify that the two were exactly identical. They had tried it before, and the results were not pretty. Suffice it to say they hadn't didn't need a DNA sample to tell the two things were not the same! Program revision after program revision had led the team to where they were now, and they thought they had it figured out. The LHC crash proved them wrong. But, now Leonard and his team were sure they'd figured out the basic problem, so here they were again. Tom and Kathy, along with a small contingent of the team, had traveled to the scanner/re-assembler site for the test.

Everything ready, Tom contacted Leonard back at DARPA and gave the go ahead. Leonard, through a dedicated link to CERN, started the software that opened the two portals. Everything looked to be going fine when the software aborted. Well, while they were hoping for a completely error free try, they didn't get very far. Leonard examined all the data printed by the error routine, and after a few minutes said, "Oh, I know where the problem is."

"Really? How long will it take to fix?"

"Just a minute. I had inserted a stop at this point in the program that I need to take out." Tom waited while Leonard deleted a single line in the software that called for the routine to stop and make sure the LHC was safe.

"There. Now let me recompile," said Leonard, and he issued the command to recompile the source code into the operational program. Then he copied it over the link to the supercomputer running the whole operation.

"OK. Ready to go!" he announced.

"Good. We still have enough time on the LHC, so let's give it another run. Let me tell the outside team." Tom picked up the handy-talky and told the team to stand by. Then he gave the go-ahead to Leonard.

He issued the command and they waited. After the right amount of time went by, the software exited. But, when it did, they got another error code. Tom picked up the handie-talkie, or "HT", as it was popularly called.

"Anything?" he asked over the link.

"Nothing," came the reply.

"What happened?" Tom asked.

Leonard was already pulling up the source code.

"I don't know," he said. "This error code is a system code, not something from the LHC software."

"Well, just what was the software doing?"

"It had to have something to do with that program branch, because we didn't get that before," he said, and began looking at the portion of the software he'd told the routine to branch to once the portals were open. After a few minutes, he began scratching his head.

"I don't know what happened, but the safety section of the software we wrote after the LHC crash 'safed' the LHC before exiting. Let me put some more checks in the system and we'll try it again."

Tom looked at his watch. "Well, take your time, because we're missing our access window. We won't have another chance until our next window next week".

Since coming back online, the LHC schedule was full and Tom's team was not what you would call a first priority.

Leonard laughed. "Yeah – I was afraid we'd run out of time. I'll put some more error checking in the software, and we'll try it again next week."

"Well," Tom said. "Another trip to the desert for nothing. OK, in the meantime, we can work more on the scalability of the non-biologic copy/reproduce mechanisms."

Tom and the team headed back to DARPA to work on the scalability. They were able to scale pretty good now, but at some point the military might want to transfer a tank or airplane or something over this thing, so they had plenty to do. Besides, they were still in the 'what-if' mode on biological transfers.

"Yeah, just sorry we couldn't make something happen today," he said.

"Right there with 'ya, brother," Tom said, "but we are sure something didn't happen, right?"

Across the country, something _had_ happened. Tom and his group would never know.

CHAPTER 12
Pasadena California

2001

Dr. Lewis Donaldson was almost asleep when there was an instantaneous bright flash and he awoke with a start and a pain on his left hip and shoulder. It was as if the couch had disappeared from under him, and he was now laying on a hard, hot surface, and he felt dust blowing in his face! As his eyes struggled to focus, he found that not only was the couch gone, but that he was sitting on his side in the dirt. Not only that, he was outside, it was dusty, and the Caltech buildings were nowhere in sight. In fact, the only buildings he saw were stone. He sat straight up with a start and found himself against the outside wall of one of the stone buildings. It took him a few minutes to make sure he was awake and not just in a really vivid dream, but when he came to that realization, he stood up and brushed himself off.

As he looked around he appeared to be on a narrow back alley between sets of block structures. Looking to his right down the alleyway, he could see breaks in the walls where there were some small simple courtyards which contained off-white clothing on ropes, apparently drying laundry. These appeared to be the back of these structures, which were, based on the clothing, possibly residential structures. The end of the alley dead ended into another larger walkway. As he was looking that way, he heard a noise to his left. Turning he saw two robed women coming his way carrying baskets. They both had head-wraps and their robes covered them head to toe, and they were both wearing sandals. As they neared him they stopped talking, then slowed down, watching him warily as they passed by on the opposite side of the alley. After passing they kept looking back at him, and finally hurried on their way. He could understand why, as he was dressed in his standard khaki pants and white dress shirt, always without a tie, so he was obviously out of place.

He watched as they rounded the corner at the end of the alley. Pausing for a few moments, he decided to see where they might be going. He walked the same direction they had gone, checking behind him as he went, and peered around the corner in their direction. This walkway was shorter, but wider, and it opened into a large courtyard where he could see some tables filled with wares being sold by men who were all also wearing robes and sandals. He stepped back against the wall, thought for a minute, then looked around the corner again. Yep, same scene. He observed and listened as best he could for a few minutes. He didn't see anyone who wasn't wearing robes and sandals, and the language he was hearing by the people near his end of the passageway was not something he'd heard before.

Just where in the world was he, and how did he get here??

CHAPTER 13
Location – Unknown

Lewis was beginning to panic a bit.

"Where in the world am I?" he thought. *"How did I get here? Who were these people? How much danger am I in?"* and the really big one - *"How do I get home?"*

Peering around the corner one more time, he pulled back and hugged the wall. He didn't know what to do. His mind was racing. *"I stand out like a sore thumb,"* he thought. Afraid someone might come down the alley and around the corner, he started back down the narrow walkway, hugging the stone and mud walls along the way. Fortunately, since this alley appeared to be the back of the dwellings, currently no one was visible. He stopped about one third of the way and leaned against the side of one of the buildings to think for a minute.

"I don't know where I am," he thought, *"but I'm definitely not in California! This must be a bad dream! OK, Lew, get hold of yourself. These people are dressed in middle eastern garb, so maybe I'm in Egypt, or Libya, or Syria, or maybe it really is just some back alley on a movie set in California! Either way, I need to figure out a way to remain incognito until I figure out what's going on. How am I going to do that?"*

The weather was pleasant - sunny in what felt like the mid seventies, basically the same weather he'd felt coming into work that morning, so he thought maybe that meant he wasn't too far away from the campus. The sun was almost directly overhead, so it must be around noon. But, there was a distinct aroma in the air of burning fires, much like you'd find in an area where homes were heated by fireplace, and it was mixed with other unidentifiable odors as well.

He looked down at what he was wearing. Nobody he'd seen in the courtyard around the corner was wearing anything like this. He looked around. Down the way a bit and across the path was a small courtyard where some robes and head-wear were hanging. Looking up and down the path, seeing no one coming, he crept over to the courtyard and 'borrowed' one of the robes, a tunic outer garment and head-wear off the vine they were hanging on and scampered down the pathway a bit. First he put on the robe and tunic. He noticed the tunic had a small draw-stringed pouch, chest high, fastened just inside the right front opening. Then he took off his shoes and socks, and put the socks in his back pocket. Next he took the shoestrings out of the shoes, tied them together, then tied each end to his shoes and slung them around his neck with his shoes just behind his armpits. Then, reaching down, he rolled his pant legs up until they would no longer be visible below the robe. Finally, he put on the headgear and arranged it like he'd seen in the movies as best as he could. His perpetual beard stubble at least kept him from having a clean-shaved face, so he thought he might be able to get by.

"Good," he thought. *"Now at least I don't stand out so much. So, what now?"*

He looked down at his bare feet. *"I need sandals!"*

He didn't have his billfold, so no credit cards, and no money. Then he remembered the change he had in his front pocket. He reached under the robe into his front pocket and retrieved 3 quarters, a dime, and a couple of pennies. *"Eighty seven cents.*

Hmm....I could have sworn I had at least dollar in change. Well, not going to get much with that. Maybe I can make some kind of deal." He placed the coins inside the small pouch and closed it with the drawstring.

He checked himself one more time, then walked back to the end of the alley. Looking around the corner, he took a better look this time. What he could see at the end of the way were at least two tables with street vendors. There were several people milling around. He stepped back, took a long breath, then headed around the corner towards the larger courtyard. Walking slowly and carefully, he stopped at the end of the passageway and leaned against the stone wall and surveyed the courtyard. There were several types of vendors here selling everything from cloth to baskets, small animals, food items, and what appeared to be very basic home utensils. There was a vendor directly across from him that had a selection of sandals with the other clothing. Lewis looked at the others in the marketplace to see how they were comporting themselves. "*I can do this*," he thought, "*I can do this - at least until I figure the situation out.*"

Taking a deep breath he, as naturally as he could, walked over to the vendor. The man was talking to someone else when he walked up so he just looked through the sandals that were on display there. He spotted a pair that looked like might fit him. He reached inside his robe and took the coins out from the small pouch. The man came over to him, and said something to him in a language he didn't understand.

"*Eich ephshar la-azor l'kha?*"

Lewis shook his head, and in a subdued voice said, "Do you understand English?"

The man just stared at him.

"Hablas espanol?" Lew asked.

The man stared at him again.

Lew tried again. "Est-ce que tu parles francais?"

The man looked at him and shook his head, not understanding what Lewis was saying.

Lewis pointed at the sandals he'd chosen, then pointed down at his bare feet.

"How much?" he said, rubbing his fingers together.

The man paused for a moment, then, perceiving what Lew was asking, said, "*Schlwoo 'sha den-ariem*".

Lewis paused for a second, pondering what to do. Deciding, he took one of the quarters he had in his other hand and handed it to the man. The man took it and looked at it as though he were examining a rare coin. He turned it over in his hand, examined the engravings on both sides, and felt of the serrated edges. The way he was examining the coin concerned Lewis. The man looked back up.

"*Yezeh zwoog mt'beh zeh?*" the man asked.

Lewis shrugged his shoulders this time. Then he picked up the sandals, pointed to them, then pointed to the quarter as he raised his eyebrows - the universal expression for "*This for that?*"

The man had a surprised look on his face. So, Lewis did it again. The man looked at the coin, then back at Lewis and a bit too vigorously nodded his head 'yes'. So, Lewis took the sandals, pulled his hands against his chest, bowed, and walked away. A few feet away, he looked back at the vendor. He was examining the coin with another man, and they seemed to be impressed. Suddenly he was afraid that might be a bad thing.

Lewis put the remaining coins back in the pouch, then went down a similar alley to the one he'd come from, sat down about a third of the way down, and put on the sandals. He could still see the crowd in the marketplace. The two men were still talking about the quarter, but they didn't seem to be anxious or mad about it, so he decided to people-watch for a few minutes. Hopefully he could see someone similar to him he would feel more comfortable approaching. He was close enough to hear some of the conversations, but he didn't recognize a single dialect.

After about twenty minutes he had come to some conclusions. First, nobody that he could hear spoke a language he could understand, or even recognize. Second, apparently no one had a wristwatch. Even in third-world countries, people wore wristwatches. Third, he didn't see anything that might be considered modern, like motorized or electronic objects of any kind - calculators for example. None of the clothing was western, though that might not be too unusual if you were in the middle east, but he had to still be in California, right? He hadn't been asleep long enough to be transported that far, had he?

This had to be a dream. But, if it was, it was the most realistic dream Lew had ever had.

CHAPTER 14
Arlington, VA

Second Decade, 2000s

Parts of the software went through yet several more rewrites as the team attempted to find out what had happened. The code was immensely complex, so identifying which section of the code needed refinement consumed a great deal of Leonard and his team's time. The goal was still to replicate a live entity from point A to point B, then back again, and hopefully do it this time without the program ending prematurely.

The time finally came to get access to the LHC again, and Tom and his team were ready for the first part of the operation. Leonard's team had finally cleaned up the part of the code that failed last time. It turned out to be an instruction that caused the software to branch to an earlier version of the code that had been written for the physical transfer, so they re-routed that instruction to branch to the correct section that dealt with the replication aspect.

All that done, the team was again gathered in New Mexico. Tom and Leonard were in the control center, and a mile away, in the first tent was a translucent container dangling from the top of the tent with the cockroach inside which would be the focus of the molecular scanner. In the second tent one hundred feet away from the first, which would be the focus of the molecular printer, an identical translucent container dangled on a string from the top of the tent. A short distance away from both tents sat two vehicles which would move in once the test was completed. Once again, their goal was to copy the cockroach in container in Tent 1 into the container in Tent 2. Kathy was in one of the vehicles, and her task was to visually verify the duplication had indeed been accomplished. If this was successful, a series of tests would be done on the two cockroaches, including an in-depth DNA analysis to prove that cockroach 2 was, for every intent and purpose, cockroach 1. If this would work, then there was no reason they couldn't just scale the parameters for larger organisms, up to and including a human being. But, that part was a long way off. Small steps....

"You guys ready?" Tom asked into the handie-talkie.

"Yep – we're ready!" came Kathy's voice over the HT.

"OK," Tom said into the HT, "here we go", and released the talk switch.

"Everything ready here?" he asked Leonard.

"Ready!" he said.

"OK, you're a go. Fire when ready, Gridley!"

Leonard gave Tom a smirk, then turned around, typed a few commands on the keyboard, and paused, looked up at Tom and said "OK – here we go!"

He hit the 'Enter' key on the keyboard and waited. The prompt went away for several seconds, then came back with the single word 'Done!' on the screen.

"Well, that's kind of anticlimactic," Tom told him.

"Yeah, I wasn't going for fancy," said Leonard. "Just functional. So, call out there and find out what happened!"

Tom keyed the HT and said, "Kathy – GO!"

It seemed like an hour went by, when in reality it was just minutes. But, everyone was on pins and needles. Tom was lifting the HT to his face to coax an update when Kathy's excited voice came over the speaker. "WE HAVE COCKROACHES!"

CHAPTER 15
New Mexico Desert

Second Decade, 2000s

The team had now been successful in replicating – actually 'translating' was probably a better term – a common cockroach from one tent to another in the New Mexico desert! Now, what about translating one from another location? So, next they tried the cockroach thing again. This time they called some people working for DARPA out in the desert not too far from where they'd put the scanner and re-assembler, had them put a tent out in their parking lot with a cockroach suspended, this time in another container from the roof of their tent, and then give them the exact coordinates where the cockroach was located.

One of the parameters they were working with was fuzzy logic. Eventually they wanted to be able to give the computer a detailed description of what they wanted to replicate, then give it an approximate time when that item would be at that location, then have the software find, isolate, and scan the object, then reproduce it at the destination location, but having the exact coordinates would be used for this series of tests. In this case, the destination would be in a tent at a remote location in Florida

DARPA used for testing with some military projects associated with NASA.

Tom called the team in Florida and told them to stand by, then muted the phone. When everything was ready, Tom had Leonard issue the commands, and they waited for the result. When the 'Done!' came back on the screen, Tom unmuted the phone on the call he had with the team waiting in Florida, and said, "SO? What do we have?"

"I am looking at something I killed in my kitchen floor last night, except this one is trapped in a box on a string!" came the reply.

"Great!!! Pack that thing up, and get it up to our lab!"

"You got it. Anything else you need from here?"

"Nope," Tom said. "You can even keep the tent!"

"Pfffft," came the reply. "It was already my tent."

"Then I guess we're finished," he said. "Thanks!"

They heard laughs on the other end, then, "OK Tom, I'll have your pest on tonight's flight."

"Thanks for your help! You guys take care," and he punched the end-call button.

A few days later, the cockroaches from both Florida and New Mexico were at DARPA, and they got the DNA tests on both and declared success. The next step would be to scale everything up and see if they could replicate larger biologics, or if the software needed tweaking. So, they went back to the two tents in New Mexico. They had proved it could be done across the continent, which meant the portal system was working. Now they just needed to know if it would scale on its own.

It turned out DARPA had a contract with a biologic medical supply outfit not too far away, and they were able to obtain some test subjects. The good part was that, since they weren't really doing anything to these biologics, they could send them back to the medical supply company when finished. Tom even wondered if they'd buy the hopefully-duplicated versions, but decided to leave that to the procurement department. Also, Tom didn't need a pet.

They started with a mouse. No problem.

Then came a rabbit. It 'multiplied'.

Next was a dog. Instant beagle. It's bark was, of course, identical.

Then it was time for the final step before trying humans. A chimpanzee. The one they had was a bit jumpy, so they gave it a mild sedative, just enough to calm it down, and gave it a try. Now they had two chimpanzees! Well, more specifically, Procurement did. Tom had no idea what they would end up doing with them.

This was as far as they were willing to go. Tom and the team could deal with a dead or even maimed animal because they could just be put out of their misery, but you can't do that with a human. He was not going down that road!

Then, they hit a roadblock. CERN pulled the plug on the LHC. It wasn't anything they'd done. They had booked a month-long project that was not only going to essentially monopolize the LHC's time, but was going to upset the schedule for everything else they had booked. It would be two months before they could get back on the schedule. So, since it was late summer, Tom told everyone they were taking a two week vacation, and instructed them to go home and not think about the project until they came back. When they did come back, they had one more major test, and then they would begin the process of turning all this over to the military as a finished project.

Tom didn't, however, take his own advice. He was concerned about what to do with the biologic replication portion of the project. They couldn't just make copies of people and let them start walking around. That would get real messy. Then there was the time-travel issue. If they send a duplicate of someone back in time, and they changed something, the ramifications were too dangerous to even consider. It would be possible to bring someone from history to the present, but to what end? By the time the team came back together, Tom had all but decided to table the biologic part of the program. Oh, they were going to finish it, but unless some intense national security issue came up, he was going to keep the biologic part under wraps – both the replicate and the physical transfer methods - until they'd had a chance to flesh out the protocols. In the meantime, they would fine tune the biologic 'replication' protocol.

CHAPTER 16
Arlington, VA

Second Decade, 2000s

The team was satisfied that the translation portion of the software was working, and had replicated a number of organisms from one place to another - both from the desert location, one tent to another, to replicating items at one remote location to another. After they got the initial glitches out of the system, it seemed to scale really well. The duplicate chimp was doing well, and their mannerisms, they found out, were almost eerily the same, to the point that if you pitched a ball to one, then to the other, they would catch the ball and make the same facial expressions. If there had been any doubt that the duplicate was, for all intents and purposes, the same as the original, time itself strangely enough had answered that question. They had even checked the sedative content in the replicated chimp's bloodstream, and found it to be exactly the same as was in the original!

That done, it was time to do some intensive testing. They had drifted away from the inanimate object replications for two reasons. First, they needed to know that the duplicate was an exact duplicate. Imagine, for instance, the military wants to duplicate an explosive device from one point to another, then blow it up. If you don't have an exact copy at the molecular level, the explosion won't go as planned. However, if the team could copy a living organism and get an exact duplicate at the end, they could be assured an inanimate object would fare well.

The second reason revolved around the idea that the military might want to, at some point, actually *transfer* troops, spies, specialists, whatever, without having to worry about borders. So, transferring living beings was really the key to prove the process worked.

Now, Tom wanted to go back to inanimate objects. He also needed to be able to duplicated in both directions. So, back to the start they went. Tom still had that original pencil! Since they had proved the system safe, they decided to forgo the trips to the desert, and he had two identical tents set up outside a bit beyond the parking lot of their facility. They set up and replicated it again. Now they had three identical pencils.

Tom had a friend who sold fireworks and had a federal explosives license, so Tom asked him to procure the largest explosive he could legally give him and to show him how to wire several of them together to make a significant bang. Tom told him it was for a party his business was throwing. Well, it kinda was! When he got it, he took the bundle outside the office and put it in the first tent, then told the system to duplicate it to the other tent on the other side of the building's parking lot. Then he went outside and set the duplicate off. DARPA security was not amused, and am embarrassed Tom had to get his boss involved. But, when it was all over, Tom told them that when we show it to the military brass, that's exactly how he wants to present it, albeit with a much larger 'bang', so the team set the timeline and benchmarks to hit to finish the project.

They also had a long philosophical discussion about the wisdom of duplicating humans. There had been a movie named

'Multiplicity' in which actor Michael Keaton played a character who 'cloned' himself multiple times to make his life less complicated. It not only made his life more complicated, but explored the idea of two duplicates living at the same time. It did not work out well.

Then there was the issue of time travel. This is when they decided that sending someone back in time – even if was just a duplicate - was too dangerous to even consider, but you could replicate someone from history forward in time. But, why would you want to do that?

So, they decided to just make it an inanimate-only project. They set up the timeline to finish the project, demonstrate it, and turn it over to the military. They would keep up development, looking for ways to make it faster and maybe add new features, but the product they would turn over would be usable, at least enough for the military to evaluate as a possible national defense tool.

Their next window with CERN came up on a Friday, and they had scheduled a two-way duplication. The goal was to copy and reproduce an item from Tent 1 into Tent 2, then turn around and make another replication from Tent 2 to Tent 1. The idea was to prove that they could, at will, copy items from one location, then copy that item back to the origin. They had to be sure the process worked both ways. There might be times, for example, when there was a need to place a surveillance or recording device at a remote location, then retrieve it, recordings intact, back at the origin. Once they had that ability, they could clean everything up, give the military a nice demonstration, and turn it over the them for evaluation and eventual deployment. With the ability to replicate and reproduce an actual duplicate, it would be a simple (relatively speaking) matter to just substitute the transfer part of the program instead of the replication portion of the program. The only difference would be that the "transfer" portion of the software would be used instead of the "replication" portion of the software. They would not, however, turn the actual transfer capability over to the military, but would hold that in reserve just in case national security left them no other choice.

Just to make things interesting, though, they decided to do this first two-way test with a biologic. That way they'd know the translation part of the software worked both ways, since any problems in that translation would be apparent upon examination of a live specimen. To keep the creepy factor down to a minimum (in case they had another of those translation errors they'd had the first few times), Tom decided to go back to their old friend, the cockroach. If something untoward happened, nobody would cry too much, they thought.

CHAPTER 17

Location Still Unknown

Lewis Donaldson stayed off to the side observing for quite a while, all the time trying to figure out what to do next. He noticed that as people would finish their business in the marketplace, many of them would leave via an opening to his left, on the opposite side from where he'd first entered the courtyard. He waited until he saw some others headed that way, and as unobtrusively as he could he followed them out the opening. It was another alley-way, though wider than the ones he'd been in before, and as he continued, others joined from other intersecting points along the way. It didn't take long until, as the passage became wider, still others entered from side passages and before long several others were headed the same way he was. He was a bit concerned someone might notice him and start asking questions, but nobody did. He just kept his head down and kept walking as nonchalantly as he could. Up ahead he could see the end of this street - he now thought of it as a street - and the closer he got the more he could see it opened into a larger area. When he finally reached it, it was a huge plaza bordered by several large structures. At the end of the plaza to his left was a large ornate building built up above the others with a fairly large column of smoke coming out of the top. It was surrounded by walls providing it with its own courtyard, and several people milled around it. There were men there wearing, of all things, swords, and some men dressed in elaborate robes and head dressings. He decided he might want to stay away from them.

Off to his immediate left leading up to the fancy building were other vendors selling small animals. Lewis wasn't interested in animals, but to his right were some small vendors selling foods. It looked like some of them were cooking meats on open stone hearths, and he was getting hungry. He was supposed to be eating right about now with the representatives from the Department of Education, but apparently that was not going to happen! So, he decided he might as well get something to eat. Lew opened the drawstrings on the pouch and retrieved the coins again. Based on what he'd been able to do with the quarter, he decided to see just how far his money might go.

Lewis sauntered up to one of the vendors, and surveyed what food he had. There was some meat, cooked fish, and some bread, as well as what appeared to be wine. He decided to pretend to be unable to speak so when one of the vendors came over to him, he simply pointed and grunted. After a few tries, he ended up with a fish, some bread, and a small rough cup-like container of wine. He took out two of the pennies and handed it to the vendor and raised his eyebrows in a "*is this good enough?*" expression. The vendor acted much like the man he'd bought the sandals from and examined each coin with wonder. It was as if he'd never seen a penny before. They exchanged glances a few times, and Lew gave him another "*OK?*" look until the vendor shrugged his shoulders and nodded. Lewis took the food and the small stone cup off to the side and sat on the steps of one of the buildings where others were eating as well.

The fish could have used a bit of lemon on it, but other than that it was pretty good, though the fact he was hungry might have had something to do with it. The bread had a bit of a strange twang to it, but the wine was tasty, though it was more grape juice than wine. With no utensils he simply ate with his hands as he saw others nearby doing the same. OK. So far so good. He finished his meal, and returned the cup to the vendor giving him a short bow with his hands clasped to his chest as he did. Now what?

For the next several hours, Lew walked around the perimeter observing what the others did, being careful to stay away from the men with swords, as well as to avoid interacting with any others. He tried not to stay in one place too long, until he noticed there were small groups of handicapped and what appeared to be homeless people who were begging for help. So, he just planted himself not too far away from them until the sun began to set. His thinking was that he'd see what they did when it was time to go to sleep, and do the same. They all finally settled down not too far from where they'd been and drifted off to sleep. Lew was exhausted, so even though he wasn't in his own bed, he found a corner to sleep in and eventually fell asleep.

CHAPTER 18

Location Still Unknown

The next morning Lew awoke, and after a few minutes, noticed two men were standing just a few feet away from him speaking in what he could only surmise was the local dialect. He just listened intently as they talked, trying to pick out something they were saying. He wasn't having any luck. Unbeknownst to him, they had noticed him and decided something was a bit off.

"Who is that man?" said the first man in the local dialect. "I have noticed him watching us as well as others. I have not seen him before."

The second man shrugged his shoulders. "I have not seen him before either, but there is something not quite right about him. Do you suppose he is to be feared, or is he just not right in the head?"

Because they were wary of him they were purposely not looking at Lew as they talked. While they were speaking another came up to them. The first man spoke in the same dialect and said, "Do not let him see you looking, but do you see the man sitting against the wall behind me? Who is he?"

The third man took a sneak look at Lew as he turned from one of the men to the other.

"I do not know who he is," he said, "but I sold him those sandals yesterday. He gave me the most curious coin as payment and I would like to know where he got it from. But, he appears to be foreign. There are a lot of foreigners in town this week."

"Show me this coin," said the second man.

He pulled out the coin and handed it to him. The second man, with his back turned to Lew, examined both sides of the coin, paying particular attention to the serrated edge as he did.

"These images are very precise!" he said. "And this edge. It must have taken an artisan hours to create it. Yet, I have never seen such a coin. It must be very valuable. Where would a man with such poor clothing get such a coin?"

"This was my question as well," said the third man. "I would like to ask him, but he does not seem to understand. He may be deaf as well. He is a strange man."

As they were speaking, Lew noticed they kept stealing glances his way. Not wanting to get in the middle of something, he rose and walked away from the area as nonchalantly as he could. The area seemed to be filling up, so it wasn't hard for him to get lost in the crowd. He went to the edge of what he could only describe as some sort of plaza he was in, leaned against a wall, and began watching those around him again. To his front was the huge ornate building, and there was still smoke coming out of the middle of the building, as there had been since he'd entered the plaza earlier that morning. People were going in and coming out in a steady stream, some dressed in well decorated robes and headdresses. There were guards in the front, though, so Lew didn't move very close in order to avoid any type of questioning.

So far, people had let him alone, but he still had no idea what had happened to him, or what he could do to get back home. He decided to reconnoiter and see if he could find anything familiar that might help him orient himself and find out where he was. So, he began walking – down through the alleys, passageways, and wide streets – anywhere that might take him to some place he might recognize. He used the smoke coming out of the big building in the plaza as a reference to keep his bearings. What he wouldn't give for a portable GPS right now!

After a couple of hours he decided three things: First, access to the city was controlled through entry and exit portals. Second, he was getting tired of carrying around his clothing under the robe he had 'borrowed', so he realized he needed someplace to stash his clothes. Finally, and the most troubling, was the area to the west of the courtyard area that not only appeared to be dangerous to go into, but there were armed men there, and they all carried swords. Not only that, the robes they were wearing, along with their capes and headdresses, brought on the worst revelation. They looked like pictures he'd seen of soldiers of ancient Rome! How could this be? As he pondered this, he realized to his great alarm that the major question was no longer "*Where am I?*" It was now "*When am I?*"

CHAPTER 19

Location And Date Unknown

The rest of the day Lew spent just wandering around observing. Whenever someone would try to engage him in conversation or ask a question, he would just act like he didn't hear them, or that he was hard of hearing. He found that nobody questioned him so long as he stay out of others' way. The longer he observed, the more he was convinced he had been thrust back in time to some era of the Roman empire. He couldn't come up with any other explanation. From his studies, and his own expertise, he recognized some of the traits of their reign, and that frightened him even more. Right now, Lew was wishing he had taken that course in Greek instead of Russian.

One thing he was sure of, though, was that he was not in Rome itself. First of all, none of the architecture indicated Roman design, and much of what he saw outside the central area of the city was inhabited by the poor. There was no other way to describe the disparity between the classes, and there was so much of a difference, with not much of what might be considered a 'middle class'.

Late in the day, he rounded a corner and saw an individual reaching into what looked like a hole in one of the structures. Lew stepped back around the corner, then peered around it to see what the man was up to. The man retrieved what looked like a cloth sack from inside the hole and just as he did, a squad of soldiers came around a corner. It quickly became apparent they'd been watching the man. His immediate impression was they were Roman soldiers, based on the tunics, helmets, and chest ornaments they were wearing. They grabbed the man, threw him to the ground, and took the sack from him. Then, one of the soldiers looked into the crevice where the sack had been stored, apparently satisfying himself it was empty, then reached down and retrieved the rock that had covered the opening and reset it so that it looked just like the rest of the wall. Then they roughly snatched up the man, and took off in the opposite direction, man and sack in tow. As they did, Lew noticed they were not as much walking as they were marching, and as they went they were shoving anyone in their path out of the way – and they were not subtle about it! It seemed as if they actually looked on the surrounding population with disdain, so they proceeded with an air of authority - or was it more arrogance? That just served as more proof of who they were. The crowd that had gathered quickly dissipated, and Lew thought this was his chance. So, he reached under his robe and retrieved his clothing, took the shoes from around his neck, wadded it all up, and quickly went to where the man had been standing. He felt the rocks on the wall until he found the one that was looser than the rest. So, he pulled it out, quickly stuffed all his clothing into the empty space, and replaced the rock.

Having done that, he looked behind him to make sure no one had seen what he'd done, then ventured off in the same direction the soldiers had gone, careful to stay what he considered a safe distance away, and tried not to draw attention to himself. He followed them for a few minutes until the squad turned a corner and disappeared. When Lew got to the corner, one of the soldiers was waiting for him. The soldier got right in his face and began yelling at him, obviously wanting to know why he was following them. Lew had the presence of mind to make gestures indicating he couldn't understand what the guard was saying, and that he might be deaf. This had worked with others throughout the day, and as he made these gestures, he began backing away and not making eye contact. The Roman came right after him yelling and after a few moments just shoved Lew and looked like he might actually attack him. Lew turned and ran the other way, and when he looked back the soldier was making "*don't ever let me see you again*" motions with his arms. Lew kept walking and when he eventually looked back again, the Roman was going back around the corner.

"*OK*," he thought, "*stay far away from the soldiers!*"

After about an hour, Lew had made a circuitous route back toward the plaza, and as he came into it he didn't see the soldiers, so he'd at least dodged that bullet.

He only had one more copper penny left, and with it he bought just enough from a street vendor to get the hunger pangs to go away. He went back to the alleyway he'd slept in the night before only to find out it was occupied, so he had to find someplace else to sleep. After another hour, he ended up on the ground under what looked like an awning made out of part of a tent. Sleep came quickly, but it didn't last. All night long as he tried to sleep, every little sound would bring fright, afraid one of the soldiers was creeping up on him, or one of the locals looking to steal something – not that he had anything they could steal – but it was a night of fits and starts. At one point he wished he still had his clothing on under the robe and tunic. The extra insulation would have helped with the night coldness. In the end, he only got about 4 hours of sleep, never more than a few stolen minutes at a time. He couldn't turn his mind off, either, and the feeling of being lost and forgotten in a land where he knew no one, couldn't speak the language, and had no way to contact anyone who could help, just wouldn't let him get any restful sleep. By the time daylight came bearing down, he was literally worn out.

"*What am I going to do?*" was the ever present thought.

He didn't have a clue.

CHAPTER 20

Location and Date - Still Unknown

Dr. Lewis Donaldson had been a prisoner in time for three days now. He was out of money, hungry, in need of a bath, exhausted from lack of sleep, and out of options. He had taken note of the destitute beggars and now felt he had no other option but to join them. They didn't seem to mind as he sat down close-by and mimicked their begging actions hoping to at least get some coins for food. In that, he had not been very successful.

The previous day the courtyard had not been as busy, as none of the vendors were working today, but there was plenty of activity at the large ornate building, though he'd seen no Roman soldiers for a while. Lew didn't know what he was going to do. Nobody seemed to speak a language he understood, nobody seemed to care that he was destitute and hungry, and worse, he still didn't know where he was or how he was going to get back home. He just sat on the steps of a stone building not too far from the ornate one with his head in his hands, and was all but on the verge of tears.

Off to his right there was a moving commotion, and apparently someone important was coming. He could see a man's head above the others, as he appeared to be riding on something, and those around him were shouting as he proceeded, waving at them.

"*Just what I need*," he thought. "*Some tin-horn politician to stir things up.*"

The man finally dismounted and disappeared in the crowd. Others seemed to be migrating that way but Lew just sat where he was. Whoever it was, he probably couldn't help, and may even be too dangerous to approach, particularly since he couldn't speak the language. Plus, as he surveyed his attire, he was not exactly dressed to meet someone important. So, back to contemplation.

As he was sitting there, head in his hands, he noticed the crowd moving slightly in his direction but still nobody took notice of him. Besides, he was dressed just like the other paupers around him, so he was literally hiding in plain sight.

Lost in thought about his plight and staring at the ground, he suddenly became aware that someone was standing before him. He slowly looked up and there, staring down at him, surrounded by much of the crowd, was the man who he had seen riding earlier!

"*Oh, no!*" he thought, as he sat up, all but terrified.

But the man simply smiled at him, then reached slowly down, grasped him by the shoulders, and carefully lifted him up, smiling at him the entire time. There was something in his eyes that settled him down and whatever fear he'd initially had subsided somewhat. As soon as Lew was standing upright, the man looked over his shoulder and motioned for someone to come forward. Another man, similarly dressed, came up and they exchanged a couple of words. The second man handed the first man something, who then turned around, took Lew's hand, placed some items in his hands and closed Lew's fingers up around them. Then the man smiled kindly at him again, and patted his shoulders. Then the man did something strange. *He winked at him*!   Then he turned around and walked away – the crowd following him.

Lew just stood there flabbergasted for a few moments and watched him as he walked away. "*Who was this man, and why me?   And what was that wink about?*" he wondered, as he watched the man and his friends walk away towards the large ornate building.

After a few moments, he remembered he had something in his hands.   He turned around so no one else could see, and looked in his hand. There were several coins he had seen others in the marketplaces using! He quickly put them in the small purse inside his robe, then turned around to see where the man had gone.   He had entered the outer courtyard of the large ornate building – somewhere Lew knew better than to try to enter.

Those around him who had witnessed the event quickly lost interest and went back to what they were doing.   Not knowing what else to do, Lew turned and went towards the street vendors. He watched them exchange coins for a few moments trying to get an idea of what his newly gifted coins might be worth, and was delighted to see that when someone used a coin similar to his, they were given several other coins back as change.   After a few more minutes watching the transactions, Lew thought he had enough of a handle on the rate of exchange to walk up and buy some food himself.

Once again, as he interacted with the street vendor, he acted as if he were unable to talk or hear. He bought some bread, fish, and more wine, waited for his change, and then went to an area behind the vendors to eat them. His stomach quickly forgave him for denying it food and soon he felt much better.

"*But this man*," Lewis thought. "*Who was he, and why me?*"

As he sat and contemplated the events that had just transpired, he came to a decision.

"*I'm going to find out who this man is, and see if I can get him to help me.*"

He got up and went back to an area where he could observe what was going on around the ornate building, hoping to see the man again.

"*This...benefactor...yes, that's what he was, a benefactor, was obviously fairly well known,*" he thought. He was sure he would see him again, and he vowed to stay in this area until he did. But, he didn't see him for the rest of the day, so he slept right there so he couldn't miss him.

The next afternoon, he saw his benefactor again, but he came in from a different direction, and Lew couldn't get him isolated enough to approach him. As a matter of fact, there was another commotion near where the benefactor was and he evidently left the area again.

Lew waited the remainder of the day – nothing.

The next day, he caught yet another glimpse again, but like before, he could not get close to him, and missed yet another chance. He tried to follow him as he left the area, but quickly lost him in the maze of intersecting streets.

Lew went back and camped out at his observation point hoping against hope that he would see the man again. He had enough funds from the man's gift to keep him fed, though he was careful to conserve in his spending. He thought he could last a few more days without having to resort to begging again, though he was sure he looked just like all the other homeless on the street.

Finally, on the fourth day, things started to happen. There had been crowds all day long and into the night in the courtyard, so it was obvious some kind of event was going on. During the night, there had been a lot of activity in and around a building between him and the ornate building's grounds and the streets remained filled with people. There were fires that were set for people to keep warm, and there was even some food floating around, so Lew, while still staying around the perimeter, at least didn't have to expend any funds to stay fed. It was almost a party atmosphere at some points during the night.

Then, around dawn, a large crowd appeared and went past him to another large building on the other side of where he was camped out. Many of those in this crowd seemed to be angry, so Lew definitely stayed out of the fray.

There seemed to be a lot of back and forth, until finally, in the building at the other end of the large courtyard, opposite the ornate one, the crowd gathered as someone began shouting. Lew went over with the rest – just another body in the crowd. Shortly, what had to be an important official based on how he was dressed, and how those around deferred to him, began addressing the crowd. He was surrounded by men in decorated robes, and by Roman soldiers.

After a few words, none of which Lew understood of course, the man motioned to others behind himself, and the soldiers brought out two bound men. To Lew's surprise, one of them was his benefactor! He would never forget those eyes. As he stood there, it was almost as if he were looking right at Lew.

It became apparent that the crowd was angry, and when asked to choose between the two men, they shouted, almost in unison, to apparently choose the other man! He was released, and Lew's benefactor was carried back into the building. In a few minutes he was brought back out by the soldiers, tied to a stake, and whipped mercilessly until he was not much more than a bloodied mess.

Now Lew was really worried. This had all happened within the last few days, and this man had gone from being welcomed and cheered, to being arrested and beaten. So much for due process, but Lew was already aware of Roman justice based on his knowledge of history.

Still, he was having trouble deducing where he was, and more importantly when he was. Since he knew the dates the Romans reigned, he knew now it had to be somewhere between 27 BCE and 476 CE, which meant he had a 500 year time period to try to fit in. He still didn't have a clue.

Then, suddenly, it all came crashing into perfect focus.

CHAPTER 21
Virginia

Early 2000s

Matthew Donaldson's interview with Davis & Jordan went so well they made him an offer on the spot. Matt had just graduated with his MBA from Yale, which certainly helped procure the offer, but it was Matt himself that closed the deal. He was personable, intelligent, well-dressed, and articulate – exactly what the people at DJ were looking for. The starting salary was attractive, and the available benefits down the road would be commensurate with his position: A company car, opportunity to travel, enticing retirement options, and plenty of vacation and personal days – all those would come in time. What more could a new grad look for? Well, a wife and family of his own to share all this would be nice, but Matt didn't think that would be in the menu of offers from DJ. He guessed he'd have to do that himself.

It wasn't that he hadn't looked, but though he'd been on several dates over the years, no one had 'clicked', and as he evaluated the possibilities in each relationship, none of them thus far had progressed beyond the girl/friend stage. He knew some of the qualities he was looking for, but he was primarily looking for someone who would share his values and love Matt just for being Matt. He didn't think he was that great of a catch, but he didn't see himself as a total dork, so he was optimistically hopeful 'she' would appear at some point. In the meantime, he wanted to put the skills he had to work and hopefully at least be successful in his business life.

Very much a 'people person', Matt had some skills you just couldn't teach. Now that he had his MBA from a prestigious university, he figured he'd have to make some really bad decisions to fail, and while he'd seen others in his own family with some questionable attitudes, they at least were making their way in the world, even if he didn't completely agree with some of those choices. His Dad always came to mind when he had these thoughts. He didn't understand some of the opinions his father espoused and they had, in large part, led to the split between his mom and dad. Despite that, his mom was doing good, and his dad was respected in his field, so there was evidence that even if you made some major wrong turns you could still find some measure of success in this world – particularly in this country.

So, Matt was on his way. He started the following Monday. The first couple of days were spent getting himself acclimated – getting an assigned parking space, filling out all the income tax and employment forms, setting up his 401K, and setting up his workspace. He was assigned a moderately sized cubicle in a room with twenty or so other similar cubicles, all surrounded by offices for those who'd 'graduated' from the cubicle jungle. That would be his first goal – get into his own office. To do that, he immediately went to work studying the company's product line.

DJ manufactured a variety of devices from printers and copiers to sophisticated lab equipment. He was assigned to the group that handled marketing, and as such he needed to know at least something about everything the company made. His goal was to be able to have a working knowledge of each product so, if he needed to, he could give what his colleagues referred to as 'the elevator speech' – a short, less that one-minute presentation on any piece that would entice a prospective client to look closer. In some cases, this 'speech' had to be somewhat technical. In others, it only needed to describe basic functions. Each of these discussions would, hopefully, pique the interest of the prospect to want to delve deeper. His people skills would fill in the gaps and, hopefully, allow him to bring in the team from a specific product line to further a sale.

Matt didn't consider himself a 'salesman' - but preferred the term 'product specialist', even though at first he wouldn't 'specialize' in any one product. But, he would be able to elicit information from a prospect, guide them to a specific product line, and the sales team could take it from there. Each sales team had a 'closer' - someone who could answer any remaining questions, overcome any objections, and eventually close the sale. After that, someone similar to Matt would be the primary contact for the client and help steer any after-sale issues to the proper people/department.

In short, Matt's immediate goal was to become a project manager – someone who would help others towards a common goal, and make a difference in growing the company he chose. Davis & Jordan could be that company, and so far, Matt liked the corporate culture, the work environment, and the people he'd met. His immediate supervisor was friendly, yet firm in his handling of issues as they came up, and clear in giving direction to others who worked under him. He was exactly what Matt wanted to be, so Matt didn't see any reason for his not occupying a similar position in the near future.

As it turned out, he was right.

CHAPTER 22
Virginia

Early 2000s

Katie graduated college with her degree in biochemistry, and accepted a position with a biochemical lab company not far from where her Dad and Mom lived. It was a good job, and the functions she looked to perform would be varied enough that the days wouldn't turn into drudgery, though she'd have to work up to that level. The company's work ranged from research support, to industrial clients, to medical testing, and they even had a couple of government contracts. In researching the company prior to joining, Katie had made sure that two of her primary criteria were met. First, nothing overly dangerous. While all biological testing contains some inherit danger, there was a line beyond which she would not go. Second, the work performed had to be ethical. She had been able to have a clause inserted in her employment contract that allowed her to opt out of any testing or research she found ethically or morally questionable, so long as she could articulate the reasons, and abide by the company's tight non-disclosure clause. She didn't see that as a problem, and the worst case would be to seek alternate employment if something came up she just couldn't live with. The company's willingness to allow that option put her at ease, so she felt, at least initially, comfortable with the employer she'd chosen.

Their workspaces were more the open concept type – no 'cubicles' – and offices were occupied by the management personnel. While those in management would make more money, Katie enjoyed the actual hands-on work, so she didn't really aspire to be stuck in an office somewhere shuffling stacks of paperwork. However, within the lab tech world, there were those who performed more of the mundane tasks, and those with more aptitude and work ethic who would be the more senior lab technicians, and would have more say in how their time would be spent. Because of her academic record, her attitude, and her soon-to-be-apparent abilities, Katie would find herself in the position she desired quicker than most.

It was a Monday, and Matt was sitting in his cubicle when he saw Jeff Morton, his boss, coming down the aisle. He paused as he came to Matt and said, "Hey Matt, you got a minute?"

"Sure," said Matt.

"C'mon in to my office."

"You got it," Matt said as he rose and followed Jeff to his corner office.

"What's up?" Matt asked as he sat down in the chair opposite Jeff's desk.

"You've been here what, a little over a year now?" Jeff asked.

"Something like that," said Matt.

"How'd you like to help man a booth at next week's micro-lab trade show in Houston?"

Matt nodded. "That'd be great. I attended the one in Boston earlier in the year just to get my feet wet, so I'd like to try my hand in the booth. What would be my responsibilities?"

"Well," said Jeff, "you've done a great job familiarizing yourself with our product catalog, and it has shown up in the staff meetings, so I'd like to see how well you do on the front lines. We'll have plenty of otherwise experienced people in the booth, so I'd like you to more or less float, talk to whoever visits the pavilion, answer questions, but call on someone else if you feel you need to. Basically see how you like it, get your 'feet wet', and when you return we'll sit down and discuss how you see your career trajectory.

Matt smiled. "So, it's a test, huh?"

Jeff smirked a bit and said, "Call it an opportunity. It's only a test if you screw it up."

Matt snickered a bit and said, "Well, I'd better not screw it up, then. I'd like that very much."

"Great!" said Jeff. "There's an initial prep meeting right after lunch in conference room A, so be there and we'll get started."

"Sounds good," said Matt. "Thanks, Jeff. I appreciate the opportunity."

"Well, like I said," said Jeff, rising, "you've done good work so far. Let's build on that."

Matt stood as well and said, "Can do, boss. I'll be there at One."

Jeff nodded and said, "Good."

Matt left, doing a pretty good job hiding the smile he had inside, and went back to his workspace to get everything squared away so he could clear his afternoon. After lunch, he met with the team in the conference room, received his personal assignments, and spent the rest of the week both in planning for the trade show, and making sure nothing would come up the following week while he was away.

Davis & Jordan had contractors that did all the construction work on their pavilion, so all the team had to do was show up and make sure all the demo equipment was in working order and set up all the paperwork displays and banners. The team flew out on Saturday to prep for the show that started on Monday. They spent the weekend preparing the space for the onslaught of attendees, most of whom would just be looking, but preparing for those who might have serious questions about the company and their offerings.

Matt was ready. He really had spent a lot of time preparing for just such an opportunity, so by the time Monday rolled around, his confidence level was high. He intended to make his mark while he was here and come away with a, hopefully, life altering reputation.

The show had been interesting the first couple of days, and Matt had just finished an in depth conversation with a prospect. He finished up his notes, went over and placed them in his folder behind the counter, and as he was turning around he heard someone just off to his right say, "So, tell me about your PCR systems and why yours are better than the ones I just saw in booth 230."

He turned and looked into a pretty, smiling face and something inside him said "*Hey – take notice*!" It took him a half-second, but he recovered quickly enough.

"Yes, PCR," he said. "I know about about the system in that other booth, and it's adequate and will do the job, but is that what you really want – adequate? If you're doing any amount of DNA testing, you'll find over the long haul our systems will be easier and somewhat faster and more capable than other '*adequate*' equipment. Hang on – let me get a brochure package."

He smiled, went over to their document station, and grabbed a prepared package on their DNA testing systems, then went back over to the counter.

"Here you go. May I ask how much testing your company does?"

"Not as much as we're planning," she said. "We've just signed a couple of new contracts, and genetic analysis, sequencing, and gene analysis are all addressed in these contracts. We might be looking to upgrade our lab equipment, and PCR upgrades are on the table."

"Well, we should have a good fit, then. Our systems are used in all those applications. Is your company a research facility, or more of a laboratory configuration?"

"Definitely a lab," she said. "Some of our clients are research firms, but we also have agreements with other entities, including a couple of government contracts. Nothing with national security implications or anything like that, but the work load seems to be on the increase."

"OK," said Matt, "gotcha. Where are you located? I'd like to make sure we get you in front of the right Rep."

"We're just outside of Philadelphia," she said.

"Really?" said Matt. "My home office is in Wilmington, so we're practically next door neighbors! Matt Donaldson," he said, extending his hand.

She shook his hand and said, "Nice to meet you, Matt. I'm Katie Reed."

The next day was the last day of the show, and Katie had spent the evening going over all the literature she'd accumulated. Back on the floor at the show, she headed in the general direction of the DJ booth, stopping a couple of times along the way to grab some brochures that she might be interested in later. As she rounded the corner she saw Matt at the counter arranging some paperwork.

"Hi, again," she said as she approached. Matt broke into a nice smile.

"Hi, Katie. So, what do you think – are we going to be seeing each other on a regular basis?"

Katie smiled and suppressed her small embarrassment, but shot right back.

"Well, that depends on you, now doesn't it?"

Now it was Matt's time to do a little suppressing.

"Yes, I guess it does," he said with a bit of a mischievous grin. "So, what do I need to do to make that happen?"

"We are talking about the PCR stuff, right?"

Now Matt, knowing he was 'caught', said, "We could be if you want. Or, I could just take you to dinner tonight and we can discuss any subject you want."

Katie laughed. "Slick, Matt." That elicited a laugh from Matt.

"Sure," Katie said. "When and where?"

"How about I pick you up at your hotel and we decide where to go together?"

"Sounds good," she said. "I'll meet you in the lobby of the Marriott just down the street."

"Six-thirty OK with you?" asked Matt.

"Yep – six-thirty. See you then," she said as she turned and went to make final visits to other vendors she'd been talking to. She was pretty sure the folks at booth 230 didn't have a shot now, though.

At 6:30 sharp, she exited the elevator and entered the lounge area of the Marriott. Matt was sitting on one of the seats directly across from the concierge counter. He stood and smiled as she came across the lobby.

"So, what are you in the mood for?" he asked.

"Well, there are lots of places to eat. But, rather than going through that dance, let's do this. What do we *not* want to eat?"

"'*Not* want to eat'?" said Matt. 'That's a new one."

"Yeah, it's something my parents used to do. You'd be surprised how many arguments about restaurants never happened, because most people are OK with saying what they don't want. Tends to narrow down the options."

"Interesting," said Matt. "OK, I don't want breakfast, and I'm not really a big fan of Mexican food. How about you?"

"OK, that helps, I'm not really in the mood for pizza, and while I like Mexican, I can bypass that easily enough. Also, breakfast? Nope."

They both laughed. "How do you feel about livestock?" asked Matt.

"Funny you should say that," she said, "because my grandparents own a large cattle farm here in Texas, so I'm a fan."

"OK," said Matt, "here's an idea. How about Japanese? Their steaks are really good, and there are a few more choices."

"Great idea!" exclaimed Katie. "I would love some sushi."

"Great – that's a plan! Let me ask the concierge what's nearby." She nodded, and they both went over to the counter. With reservations made, they left in Matt's rental and headed for dinner.

The evening went very well, and they spent a couple of hours getting to know each other. When they returned to the Marriott, Matt gave Katie a hug.

"I have enjoyed this," he said. "How do you feel about an encore when we're both back on home turf?"

"I'd like that," she said, and took out a notebook from her handbag, wrote her name and contact information, and handed it to Matt. "Call me when you get back home and get your feet back on the ground, and we'll do this again."

Matt smiled. "Here," he said as he took one of his business cards and wrote his personal information on the back. "OK, the front is if you have any questions about business. The back is for anything else," and he handed it to her.

"Great! See you when we get back home."

"You, too," he said, and gave her one more hug. He thought about a small kiss, but decided to save that one for their next date.

"G'night, Katie," and with that she headed in the Marriott, and he went back to his car and drove towards his hotel. They both had smiles on their faces.....

Matt's first show had been very successful both for Davis & Jordan, and for him. He had spent all week contacting all those he'd talked to at the show – answering questions, arranging appointments, generally doing all the follow-ups you would do with new prospects. There had been plenty of interest in the company's offerings, and they were becoming well known in the community that would use the products in DJ's line. From what Matt had seen and observed, the company was reputable, and not only did he have no issues with the way DJ did business, but was taking pride in not only the company itself, but the people he worked with. That's not to say that there weren't a few questionable individuals in the hundreds of people that worked for the company, but that would be true for any organization. In his opinion, though, DJ was a company anyone should be proud to be associated with.

His contact list was robust, and it had taken him all week, and he was almost done. It was late Thursday afternoon, and he only had one person left on his list for the week.

The phone on Katie's desk rang with that distinct tone that indicated an outside call, rather than an inter-office one, so that kicked her into customer mode.

"This is Katie. How may I help you?"

"Hi, Katie," said the voice on the phone. "It's Matt from last week's show." Katie smiled.

"Oh, hi, Matt. I see you're back to work, too."

"That I am, Katie. I'm doing my follow-up calls this week, and I've saved the best for last."

Katie smiled again. "Oh, really? Or, am I the last call on your way out the door?"

Matt laughed and said, "Well, if I ever gave you that impression, I'm going to have to reassess how I relate to people!"

Katie chuckled at him. "No – you did just fine. But, I guess this means I can make you late for dinner, then, right?"

"Any time, Katie," Matt said, "any time."

They both laughed and Matt continued, "So have you had a chance to look over the literature I gave you at the show?"

They talked about Matt's product line, particularly the PCR equipment, and DNA processing in general. As they were wrapping up, it was obvious to both that further conversations on pending acquisitions were necessary.

"Well, then," said Matt, bringing the subject to a decision point, "tell me what your calendar looks like and I'd like to come by, meet with you and your staff, and see if we can find a good fit for your company's requirements."

Katie looked at the calendar she kept on her desk. "Well, I have client meetings most of next week, so how about you let me get through those, because that may give us a better idea of exactly what we're going to need and when we're going to need it."

Matt made a note on his scheduler to call her back next Thursday. "That sounds like a plan. I'll call you same time next week and we'll set something up for the following week."

"That'll work for me," said Katie.

"Great," said Matt. "On a non-related note, how do you feel about dinner tomorrow night? I enjoyed talking to you at the show, and I'd like to see you and not talk about DNA testing or lab equipment."

"I'd like that," said Katie with another smile. "How do you want to meet."

"Tell you what," said Matt, "I will email you what I don't want to eat, and you pick a restaurant, email me the address, and I'll meet you there. How does eight sound?

Katie laughed. "That also sounds like a plan. I'll expect a list of stuff you don't like, then."

"Well, I didn't mean for that to sound negative," Matt said. "I'd like to start off on a positive note."

Katie chuckled again and said, "Oh, it has Matt. Don't worry. I await your email."

With that, she gave him her email address and they hung up. In less that two minutes Katie had an email from Matt.

Picking a restaurant was easy. All Matt had sent her was '*All you need to know is that I am NOT a vegetarian!*" So, she picked a nice place somewhat in between where they both lived, and when she arrived at the restaurant, Matt was waiting for her. They had a fine meal and got to know each other better. As it turned out, the connection they'd felt at the show was still there. When they left, neither was ready for the night to end, but Matt had prepared for that.

"Have you ever seen the area from a helicopter?" he asked.

"A helicopter?" she replied, a bit surprised. "No, can't say I have. I've only seen it from an airliner. Have you?"

"Nope," he said, "but I have a friend who flies commuter flights for executives, and I have him on standby. How do you feel about a little air adventure before we call it a night?"

The surprise on her face said it all. "I'd love that!"

"Great!" said Matt. "Leave your car here and I'll call him and tell him we're on the way."

That garnered a wide smile. "Okayyy," she said, "that sounds interesting!"

Matt pulled out a cell phone and called his pilot friend. They arranged to meet at the airport in thirty minutes, so Matt hung up, and said, "He's set. Let's go."

Roughly a half hour later they pulled up to the airport's heliport and there was a sleek commercial helicopter with a man in his mid thirties in full uniform waiting at the side with the door open.

"Katie, this is Bill. He flies this thing all week long ferrying bigwigs back and forth. He and I went to school together, and I can personally vouch for his flying abilities. Bill, this is Katie. She's your VIP for the evening."

Bill extended his hand and shook Katie's, then shot an approving glance over at Matt.

"Your carriage awaits, M'lady," he said as he motioned for her to step up into the passenger compartment. "You, too, I guess," he said to Matt with a smirk.

"M'lady, huh? What about M'Lord for me?"

"Dream on, peasant."

They all laughed as Matt stepped in and Bill closed the door. They buckled in, and put on their headsets so they could talk over the blade noise as Bill got in and started it up. With a few words to the control tower, he said over the intercom, "You guys ready?"

Matt glanced at Katie. She gave him a thumbs up with a big smile, and Matt said "Yep – let 'er rip!"

"My, how casual we've suddenly become," said Bill with a chuckle. "OK, here we go."

He increased the speed of the motor and with a last check of his instruments and a safety look around, he gently pulled up on the collective and the sleek machine rose from the ground. Around fifty feet off the ground, he rotated the craft to the North and deftly transitioned from a hover to forward movement, gaining altitude all the while.

"Wow, that was smooth," said Katie.

"Thanks," said Bill. "I try to make these transitions as smooth as I can. From here, we'll go a bit to the Northeast. We'll stay west of the river until we get near Philadelphia, then circle around up near Ridley Creek park, then circle back towards Wilmington, then back to the airport. If you have anything you want to see on the way, let me know. This aircraft has a GPS navigator that will guide us wherever we want to go."

Matt looked over at Katie. She was fascinated with what she was watching out of the window.

"Can you fly over my house?" she asked.

"Sure – give me your address."

She gave it to him and he punched some numbers into an onboard GPS.

"OK, I have the route. Just sit back and enjoy your trip. I'll point out some things to look at as we go."

For the next several minutes Matt and Katie watched the world below them as the aircraft flew towards Philadelphia. Every so often Bill would point something out on one side of the aircraft or the other. As they approached the Philadelphia area, Bill said, "I'm going to stay outside the approach lanes for the Philadelphia airport, then circle around to your house. I'll let you know when we're close."

"Great!" said Katie. "This is amazing!" and she shot a joyful glance at Matt.

Bill's maneuvers were as he described, but smooth, and had she not known what he was doing, she probably wouldn't have noticed.

"You're really good at this," she said over the intercom to Bill.

"Well, I have a pretty demanding clientèle, so I've had a bit of practice", he said.

A couple of minutes later, he came back on.

"OK, you should start to recognize some of the area now. Let me know if you see anything you're familiar with."

She began looking intently at the ground. "Oh! There's the shopping center! I know where we are!"

Then, suddenly, she grabbed Matt's shoulder and pulled him towards the window on her side of the craft.

"There! That's my apartment!", and she pointed to a building situated in the curve of a street a couple of blocks over from a big shopping center.

"Man, they really need to wash that roof!" she said. "I had no idea that thing looked so nasty from the air."

"Good. Now you've got something to hold over your landlord," Matt said with a grin.

"Hey, Bill. How close can you get to the top of one of these buildings?" she asked.

"Well, in a residential area, as long as I have plenty of horizontal clearing, I can get as low as 1,000 feet without violating any regulations. You want me to get closer to your apartment?"

"Nope!" she said. "But I have another idea. Do you know Morse code?"

CHAPTER 23
Virginia

Early 2000s

"Dad, you're not going to believe it!" exclaimed Kelly.

Tom had answered the phone to find his eldest daughter on the other end. Kelly was the creative one in the family, and had started her own photography business. Though it had been a rocky start, she was doing rather well now.

"What am I not going to believe?" he asked with a laugh.

"First, get Mom on the extension," she said.

"OK, hang on", and with that Tom yelled to Kathy to get on the phone. "Kelly has something to tell us."

In a couple of seconds he heard Kathy pick up the extension.

"OK, I'm on. What's up?", she asked.

"Well, apparently, Kelly has some news, and she seems to be excited about it," he explained. "Kelly, we're both on now. What's up?"

Kelly began. "You know I was telling you about some work I did for a man in Manhattan?"

"Sure," said Kathy on the extension.

"Well, I got a call from him today," Kelly began, "and he was really impressed with the photos I took, and the way I presented them. Evidently he works for a magazine and he took them to his editor. They want to meet me about doing a photo layout at Giraffe Manor in Kenya!"

"Kenya?" asked Kathy incredulously. "What kind of layout?"

"Well," Kelly began, "there's a small village there one of their reporters has visited, and she wants to go back and do a full story on them, and I'm going to do the photo layout."

"That's wonderful!", said Tom. "When is all this happening?"

"That's what the meeting is about," Kelly said, "but that's not the most exciting part.   The photo layout is for National Geographic!"

Tom and Kathy were speechless for a moment.

"Wh...who was this guy?" Tom asked.

"His name is Norman, and it turns out he works for them out of their New York office. The work I did was for him personally, but he liked it enough he showed it around, and next thing you know, I'm getting a call from their assignment editor asking if I'd be interested."

"Well?" asked Kathy. "Did you say 'yes'"

"I said yes to the meeting," Kelly said, "but they haven't actually offered it to me yet."

"If their asking for a meeting," Tom said, "there's a good chance they're going to ask you. Do you want to do this?"

"Do I want to do this?" Kelly asked incredulously. "Of Course I do!!"

That brought a laugh from both Tom and Kathy. They all talked about the possibility of the trip, the logistics, how much it would pay - the inoculations - and after Kelly had allayed their fears about any dangers, real or imagined, they finally ended the call, with both Tom and Kathy telling Kelly how proud of her they were.

Tom and Kathy Reed both talked about Kelly's news and how thrilled they were of her, and after a few minutes went back to relaxing in their living room watching a movie they had on a DVD. It had been a long day at the office, and an exciting evening with the call from Kelly, and they were both spent, so they'd finally literally 'crashed' on the couch. It was a good thing they had stopped and bought take-out so Kathy didn't have to fool with supper, and now the only real issue they faced was whether they could make it though a long movie without going to sleep. Tom was sure this would not be a late night, because neither of them would last that long.

He looked over at Kathy, reclining on the other side of the couch with her feet in Tom's lap. Her eyelids were beginning to fade.

"Are you going to go to sleep on me?" he asked.

"Anything's possible," she muttered. "I'll try to make it through, but if I don't just let me lie here."

"Yeah, I might be persuaded to join you," he said with a grin.

She turned her sleepy head in his direction. "Do you want to just call it a night?" she asked.

"I'm thinkin' about it..." he said, but just then he stopped and craned his head a bit.

"What?" Kathy asked.

"Do you hear something?" he asked.

She listened for a second, then said, "Yeah. What is that?"

"Sounds like a helicopter," Tom said, getting up from his end of the couch. He stood for a second, listening, then headed for the living room window.

"It seems to be getting closer," he said peering out the window. "I wonder if it's a Medivac or something. We generally don't hear those things around here."

Their house was in the middle of a large residential area, and there were no airports or significant office buildings nearby, so an aircraft in their vicinity was unusual. As a matter of fact, Tom couldn't remember hearing one from inside the house.

As he was peering out the window, a bright light suddenly lit up the front yard. Kathy saw it and jumped up off the couch.

"What tha.....", Tom said as he headed for the door, Kathy right behind him.

As they emerged from their house onto the front lawn, the helicopter began hovering over their house. A couple of their neighbors had emerged from their homes and were looking up at the craft as well. Then, the light on the bottom of the helicopter began blinking.

"That's Morse!", exclaimed Tom. The quick blinks were dots, and the longer ones dashes.

"Dot-dot-dot-dot, dot-dot," muttered Tom. "They're sending 'Hi'! That was sent 3 more times, then the message changed....Tom began translating the characters one by one as they were sent.

"*EIGHT....EIGHT*. Eighty-Eight!" said Tom with a grin. "Somebody's playing with us...who would be sending the shorthand for 'love and kisses' from a helicopter?"

Then the light began sending different characters....Tom once again translated.

"*D....E........K...A...T...I...E*. IT'S KATIE!" he said with a laugh. He and Kathy began waving with both arms. After a few seconds of their waving, the last message was sent, and Tom once again translated.

"*S....K*. OK, 'End of transmission'," said Tom and they once again both waived. As they did, the craft rose and veered away, flying off in the direction from which it had come.

120

"What in the world is Katie doing in a helicopter this time of night?" asked Kathy.

"Your guess is as good as mine," said Tom, "but she certainly owes us an explanation."

One of his neighbors across the street yelled over at Tom.

"What's this all about, Tom?"

Tom walked towards him along his driveway and they met in the street. "That was my daughter, Katie. I don't know what she's up to, but she had the pilot send me the Morse code for 'Love and Kisses, from Katie'. Woke us up from a movie we were almost sleeping through."

His neighbor laughed. "Well, tell her she woke up the whole neighborhood. I though someone was about to get abducted or something."

Tom laughed. "At least it wasn't a black military helicopter. THAT would have been bad!"

As they were talking other neighbors joined in the conversation, along with Kathy who had followed Tom. Needless to say, Katie had made a bit of an impression on more than just her parents. She really was going to have to do some explaining now….

The weekend after the helicopter incident, Katie invited Matt over to her parent's house for Sunday dinner. Tom had all but insisted that he wanted to meet the guy who'd buzzed his house with a helicopter, and told Katie to 'play up' the mock anger with the invitation to see Matt's reaction when he showed up. Matt, though, was not that intimidated, and it didn't take long for him to become comfortable around Katie's parents. Once the good impression was cemented, they all had a good laugh about the 'copter incident.

"Maybe you could get your guy to take us up sometime," said Tom during the meal. "I've been up in one once, but Kathy never has. What do you think?"

"Well, I'll gladly ask him," replied Matt. "We were in college together, and he frequently has some empty trips when he's ferrying some big-wig to or from someplace, and since he owns the company, he pretty much decides when and where he flies. Let me see what I can do."

"Great!" exclaimed Kathy. "I'm in!"

"I'll set something up," said Matt.

"So, where'd you guys go to college?" asked Tom.

"Well, it's funny," said Matt. "Bill and I both were roommates at UCLA, and we both ended up here on the East Coast. He did a stint in the Army flying choppers and finished out his tour at Fort Meade. He became friendly with some of the higher ranking officers there, which then translated into some contacts after the service. Hence, the executive transport gig. I'm here because my parents both wound up here. Mom and Dad had a rocky start early on, but they're both fully committed now to each other."

They spent another hour just exchanging personal and family histories, and around 3:00, Matt and Katie left for the trip home. After they left, Tom settled down in the living room to watch the Braves game on TV while Kathy finished up in the kitchen. Finally, she came in the den and reclined in the matching recliner that was 'hers'.

"So," she asked, "what did you think of Matt?"

"Oh, I like him," said Tom. "He and Katie seem to fit together well. There might be something there."

"Oh there is," said Kathy, "I think we're going to be seeing a lot of Matt."

"I'm OK with that," said Tom. Then, the crowd in Atlanta on TV began to go wild over a grand slam in the bottom of the first inning.

"I'm pretty OK with that, too!" laughed Tom.

Katie and Matt had been dating for nearly a year now. While one didn't necessarily have anything to do with the other, Katie's company had seen the value in the lab equipment from DJ, so in addition to their personal relationship, Matt was the primary contact for Katie's company, which gave them plenty of contact, now both on a personal and a business relationship.

CHAPTER 24
Middle East

Somewhere Back In Time

They took the bloodied mass that just a few hours ago had been a man welcomed and cheered by many, but now was a prisoner of the Romans, who ridiculed and harassed him mercilessly as they took him back into the large building, Lew was amazed he was walking at all.

The sun had been up for a while now, and the crowd was growing by the minute. Lew had spent enough time the last few days in the main courtyard to feel comfortable with the way things were done, as long as he stayed away from the soldiers. Even the larger crowd today didn't give him too much pause, because he'd learned to 'disappear' in the masses. However, even though he felt reasonably safe, he had to be on his guard every minute.

There was a commotion near the entrance to the large building as the Roman soldiers started parting the crowd, and they were not gentle about it. Something was about to happen, and Lew wanted to see what the deal was.

The soldiers quickly made a path, but Lew was too far back in the crowd to see what was going on at the entrance, so like most of the rest, he waited to see what would happen. It didn't take long.

Some people starting shouting, and Lew finally saw someone coming down the path. The first man Lew saw was led by a Roman guard and he was carrying something. There was his benefactor, still bloodied and barely able to walk, because in addition to his injuries, he was now carrying a.....a large wooden cross! Lew was stunned. Not only that, behind him were two other men, both also carrying crosses

Now, while Lew was an atheist, he had heard the crucifixion story, and knew enough to realize that's what he was looking at. "*So, OK*," he though to himself. "*I concede that this Jesus actually existed, so this is not a deal breaker*."

But, he had not expected the Biblical account to be this accurate, and this...this...*real*. As he watched the procession of the soldiers, the three men, the crosses, he ended up just following the crowd as they made their way through the narrow streets towards the northern part of the city. He wanted a better look.

Lew started progressing in the crowd but wasn't getting any closer, so he took a different approach. He scurried down a side alley until he reached a cross-way of an intersecting walkway and took a right. He all but ran down that way until he came upon another intersecting alley. Again he took a right, brushed past those gathered in that passage, and ended up at a place a few yards ahead of the procession where the street opened up a bit. As he looked down the street where the procession was coming his way, he saw the man he now believed to be Jesus spurred on with whips by the Roman guards to the shouts of the crowd. Not everyone, though, was shouting. Some were weeping, while others just looked stunned by the sudden reversal of fortune.

Suddenly, Lew could not believe what he was seeing, as Jesus stumbled and fell to the ground under the weight of the cross. The Romans yelled at Him and He tried to get back up, but He was just too weak and couldn't handle the weight. One of the Roman guards went over to the crowd, grabbed a man, and forced him to come pick up the cross, and finally the procession continued.

Lew had a problem. In his mind, this man was nothing more than flesh and bone just like he was. But, he remembered his grandmother's stories about Jesus, the man he was looking at right now, who had performed some things that some might consider magical. At least that's what he thought, and while he also wasn't necessarily a believer in magic, he was desperate, and this was a grasping-at-straws moment for him. So he had a decision to make. If this guy really could perform magic, or whatever it was, he might be able to help Lew get back home. As they neared his position, his desire to return home over-rode his beliefs to the point that he suddenly darted out to where the prisoners were.

"If you're who you say you are, help me get back home!" he yelled as he approached. He didn't get far.

One of the Roman soldiers saw him come running out into the street and caught him mid-yell, punched him in the stomach, and just bowled him over. Then he took a whip he had at his waist and started to whip Lew. Lew jumped up just in the nick of time and ran back down the alley, knocking over a couple of people on the way. He went pretty far before looking back to see if the soldiers were chasing him. They weren't. It took him a few moments to recover, as he discovered the soldier had actually punched the breath out of him. As he recovered, and pondered what to do, it occurred to him that they were taking him not too far away, so maybe he'd have another chance.

It took him a while to find out where they had gone, but even though he was all but lost, he listened for the sound of the crowd and used that as a guide. Soon he heard the ruckus just beyond one of the city walls, so he mixed himself in part of the crowd going there and wound up on a hillside. As he topped the hill, he saw Jesus and the other two men. The soldiers had stripped them naked, and they were just finishing nailing the last nail in His hands. As he watched in horror, they lifted up the heavy cross and dropped it into a waiting hole with a thud. Jesus cried out in agony as the sudden jolt just tore at His feet and hands where they were nailed into the wood. The same happened to the other two, one on each side of Jesus. They were all three hanging on wooden crosses, the Roman soldiers at their feet!

CHAPTER 25
Jerusalem

Around 30 AD

Unable to approach the trio hanging before him, all Lew could do was watch. The soldiers were having a field day as they taunted Jesus. Three of them began a small argument about the clothing Jesus had been wearing, and decided, evidently, to gamble for them. There were agonizing groans and cries from the crosses, as each one had to physically lift himself up with his nailed feet to get a breath. At one point Jesus, in the middle cross, said something to His captors, and they offered something up to Him on a rag, which He refused, blood trickling down His face from what appeared to be a thorny headpiece they had slammed down on His head.

They had been on their crosses for a couple of hours when Jesus said something to a small group, obviously friends and/or family, who were understandably distraught. One of them, a man who had been comforting the women, grabbed one of the oldest of the women and hugged her tightly as they both cried.

All this time, the sky had grown increasingly dark. Normally it would signal a coming thunderstorm, but Lew had never seen darkness such as this. It was as if the clouds were very high in the sky, but very black. So black, that it reminded him of a solar eclipse he'd seen several years ago in South America. The sun had still been there, but you could see the stars in the sky off to the side. In this case, there were no stars, no sun, no moon – only darkness. The Romans appeared to have the same observation and were ready to get it over with and decided to put an end to things. As they were making this decision, the Man in the middle, the one Lew had decided was the historical Jesus, looked up, said something in a loud voice that Lew, of course, didn't understand, then hung His head and went limp.

The soldiers made their decision, then went to the two on each side of Him and used a mallet to break the bones in their legs. It was horrendous. Lew almost threw up, and couldn't even look at them any more. While they were expelling their last breaths due to the inability to move into a breathing position, the soldiers went up to Jesus to do the same, but noticed He was no longer breathing. One of them took a spear and shoved it in His side causing His internal fluids to run out on the ground. That's when Lew lost the contents of his stomach. The Man was dead. It was all over.

Suddenly, the earth began to shake, and the sky was so dark it was as if the sun was no longer shining. Lew didn't do the actual math, but he was sure the odds of an earthquake and an eclipse happening at exactly this moment were, literally, astronomical.

As the soldiers, keeping a watch on the sky, hurriedly took the bodies down from the crosses, Lew wasn't sure what to do. He had hoped for some help from this Jesus, but that wasn't going to happen. He began to wander away, as did the rest of the crowd. He wasn't paying any attention to where they were all going because he was deep in thought, and profoundly affected from what he had just witnessed. The sky was still dark, but the earthquake, strangely, had no aftershocks, so he hoped that was over.

He stopped and looked back at the scene. The soldiers had removed the bodies and were carrying two of them away. But, the third, the body of Jesus, was being carried away by someone else. The first two were carried in one direction, while the third was wrapped by these men and carried down the hill on the far side. Lew wanted to see where they were taking it, but they quickly disappeared down the hill which was too far away for Lew to get there in time. Besides, the soldiers were pretty much all over the place, and possibly fearing trouble, Lew once again was unsure what to do.

Just then he saw one of the men who had been seen with Jesus on that first day, the same man he'd seen Jesus talking to earlier from the cross. He was comforting an elderly woman and two younger ones as he escorted them back towards the city. Lew suddenly remembered that some of the stories his grandmother told him from the Bible made the claim that Jesus had actually come back to life, so he decided followed them just to see what actually happened. He stayed far enough away they didn't suspect him, and besides, he looked like just another vagabond living on the streets.

He followed them to a small adobe-like structure a little piece from the city where he noticed some of the others he'd seen around Jesus that day. Wanting to remain unobtrusive, he stayed a half-block away in the corner of an alleyway where he could see the comings and goings into the building. For the rest of the night, only a couple of more individuals entered the structure, and no one left. After another night of fitful sleep he awoke the next morning early, and watched from the alleyway all day. He had some bread and a flask of wine he'd bought the day before, and while he was hungry, this was enough to sustain him. Again no one left the structure.

The next day was the same, so he kept watch, again into the night. As the third night approached, it seemed as if this was a futile effort, so he decided that if nothing happened tonight, he would go over, knock on the door, and just find out what the deal was. So, he went to sleep.

Just after dawn on the third day, as the sky was just beginning to get brighter, Lew was awakened by the sound of women's voices heading his way. He just ducked his head and pretended to still be asleep as they walked by. Then he looked and recognized one of the women as having been in the building with the rest. Lew was trying to decide if now was the time to make his move or not when suddenly the ground began to shake.

Someone came to the door just as the quake began to subside, looked over the surroundings for a second, then went back inside. Once more, Lew was about to make his move when from behind him one of the women came running up and went inside where the others were. She wasn't in there long when two of the men and the woman came running out of the building and past Lew. A few minutes later, two more of the women also went in the same direction the others had gone. This time he followed. As he started to round a corner, the two men came running back, so he just kept going straight until the men, not noticing who he was, were running in the opposite direction. He was about to go back in their direction, when two of the women also came around the corner and went in the same direction as the men had gone. So, he waited another minute or so, then went back to his observation area, hoping to figure out what they were up to.

For the rest of the day, there were numerous comings and goings from the dwelling. As Lew watched, he was now less sure that a direct confrontation was the way to go. Then he again remembered his grandmother's stories about Jesus reappearing, and while Lew knew that was impossible, now he just wasn't sure this hadn't all been a ruse. Hoping again to be helped, he decided to follow and observe these men and hope to find out exactly what the truth was. Besides, what else was he going to do? It wasn't like he had a job waiting or anything, and time, for him, was plentiful right now. So he waited, followed, and observed.

A few days later, all of the group appeared to be gathered again in another home not too far from the first place, but again, nothing other than a meeting, though when they began coming out of the dwelling, there seemed to be a mood change. For some reason they were no longer cowering and afraid of their own shadows as they had been before the incidence after the second earthquake.

The men had finally noticed Lew skulking about, but since he appeared to be just another street beggar, they paid him little attention. Unbeknownst to him, they had already had a conversation about him.

Two of them were walking to the market to obtain food, when one spoke to the other in the local dialect. "Do you see that man behind us?"

"Yes. He has been around a lot recently. Who is he?"

"I do not know, but he does not appear to be dangerous. Should we invite him to join us?"

"I would say no at this time, until the Master gives us more instruction. But there is no reason to fear him so much as I can tell."

"I agree. But, let us watch him closely. Perhaps ask the Master what to do in such cases."

"Agreed."

They bought the food necessary for the day, and on the way back noticed the man sitting along the side. One of them stopped, looked at the man as he would any other beggar, and offered him some food. The man seemed surprised, but when the man smiled at him Lew nodded his head and carefully approached them. They handed him some bread, a piece of fish, and a small leather flask of wine.

Lew was a bit taken aback, but realized they thought he was just a beggar, so he took the food, clasped his hands to his chest, and bowed quickly, and retreated to the side of the road, turning one last time to bow once again and nod his head. The men smiled and went their way. Since Lew knew where they were going, he stayed behind until he'd eaten the bread and fish. Then he took the flask with him and returned to his perch a couple of hundred feet down the alley from where the others were.

From that point on, Lew would stay in sight of the men, never approaching them, but keeping watch over what they were doing, and every so often one of them would pass a bit of food and drink over to him. Once, one even tried to engage him in conversation, but Lew feigned deafness and inability to speak other than in grunts, so eventually they thought of him as their personal charity project, even though Lew never really tried to join their group.

Lew let them, because he really had no other options. He couldn't speak their language, and they couldn't speak his. Besides, even if they could understand each other, they would never really understand what he was asking for.

CHAPTER 26
Jerusalem

Around 30 A.D.

There was a flurry of activity in the house where the supporters of Jesus were, well, *headquartered* for lack of a better term. There seemed to be a new frame of mind with these people. Where just a few days ago they were bemoaning the loss of their friend, today there were smiling faces and a spring in their step. Lewis wasn't sure what was going on, but he was at least getting the crumbs from their table. Periodically, one of them would invite him, it seemed, to eat with them, but each time he refused. He kept to himself and subsisted on their handouts, and they were as generous as they could be with him. If this was what being a pet was like, it wasn't so bad.

But, here was the problem: Lew had been here a couple of weeks now, and he was no nearer finding out what happened to get him here, or more importantly, *if* there was any hope of his getting back home. He had been scheduled to be out of town at a conference for a week, but that would have ended a week ago. He wondered if they were searching for him. He wondered what had happened with the grant. He wondered who was teaching his classes. He wondered what his daughter thought! If he did get back, how would he explain his absence, and how would he ever get his life back on track?

Every time he thought of these questions, he slid into another psychological slump, and these depressed moods were coming periodically. He was alone. There was no one to talk to, and the people who did seem to care, while they treated him well, would never be his friends because they couldn't even communicate on a basic level. Eventually he'd snap out of his depressed mood, but generally that took at least a good night's sleep.

CHAPTER 27
Jerusalem

Around 30 A.D.

Lew had been here over a month now, and he was not getting any closer to finding a way home. While the charity of the followers of Jesus had been helpful at first, Lew needed more than crumbs to keep fed. He had turned to begging and discovered he was not too bad at that. One day he stumbled on some old fishing nets and spent the afternoon repairing them enough that he was periodically able to catch a few fish. He was then able to trade some of the fish for bread, wine and other foods prepared by street vendors and others. That, his begging, and the little bit of food Jesus' followers would pitch him kept him nourished enough that he actually gained back a bit of the weight he'd lost those first weeks. He had even found a small cave where he made a bed out of straw that, to him, was a good as any five-star hotel compared to sleeping on the ground. Mimicking how the women took care of their robes, he was able to sneak off often enough to keep his garments cleaned without anyone around to see. He longed for his original clothing, but he knew if he wore his actual clothes, there would be questions. So, he just remained in his *borrowed* attire.

To his astonishment, once he thought he'd seen someone who looked like Jesus but He was very far off, so Lew just attributed it to wishful thinking. On another occasion he had trailed one of the followers of Jesus to a large crowd of people listening to someone who looked just like Jesus, but by the time he could get anywhere near, He and his closest confidants were gone. That was the last he'd seen. The men, who he now thought might be what the Bible had called His disciples, had changed. They were now men who seemed to be on a mission. Well, Lew thought he could understand that. But, where did that leave him?

One day, while at a place just outside the city where Lew was washing his clothing, he noticed another man not too far away who was doing something strange. He would dip something in the water, then bring it back up to his face for a few seconds, then start the process again. Suddenly Lew realized the man was *shaving*! What Lew wouldn't give for a shave and a haircut, but there were no barber shops anywhere around.

As he watched, he made a decision. He had a tunic that had been given to him, but was also too small for him, so he walked over to the man. When the man noticed him, Lew made a gesture with his hands on his face like he wanted to shave, again feigning the inability to speak. The man just looked at Lew, so Lew took the tunic, offered it out to the man, then again made the gesture with his hands on his face. Apparently the man deciphered the pantomime Lew was getting more and more proficient with, and nodded his head. Lew handed him the tunic, and the man handed Lew the device he was using to shave himself. Lew quickly examined the device, noticing it was apparently some carefully selected pieces of glass that had been fitted into a rudimentary handle.

Lew smiled, then reached down to the water, cupped some in his hands, wet his beard, and began to shave as best he could.

He was able to use the water as a makeshift mirror, and when he finished, he wasn't too dissatisfied with the result. He was a bit surprised at how close to his face he'd been able to crop his beard.

However, he also noticed his hair had become very long and frayed, so he then wet his hair, and used the 'shaver' to cut his hair. The man who'd lent him the tool looked on with amusement, at which Lew just shrugged his shoulders and finished the job. Looking in the water 'mirror' one last time, Lew was not unsatisfied with the result, but he was certain he'd not be receiving any job offers as a barber! So he handed the 'shaver' tool back to the man, who just shook his head, and pointed to the cloak. Lew again made his patented "this for that?" gesture, to which the man nodded and smiled. Lew smiled back, then clasped his hands to his chest and bowed to the man, then turned and walked back to where he had been washing his clothes.

Just one more day Lew would never be able to explain.

CHAPTER 28
Jerusalem

Around 30 A.D.

A few days later, the city was starting to fill up with people again. Lew wasn't really sure what all the celebrations were, but this had all the makings of another one. He had noticed these disciples had gathered in a house where they'd been together many times before. They had been in there for a while, but that had always been the case, so in that, this was not unusual.

Lew was sitting in his normal distance, about fifty feet away from the house where they were, feigning his persona as a beggar. This had worked out well for him. Most people didn't pay attention to him, since there were many beggars in the city during such celebrations, and it gave him a way to keep watch on the group while at the same time garnering some food along the way. Some people would give him change, but many would simply share their food with him. It wasn't a lot, but with what the disciples gave him, and what he was catching, it kept him sustained.

A man had just given him a coin when suddenly there was a rumble so loud that everyone stopped what they were doing and looked around. It was hard to tell where it was coming from. There were no clouds in the sky, the wind was relatively calm, and to Lew it sounded just like a jet had come over, so instinctively

Lew looked up in the sky searching for aircraft. For some reason, though, it seemed to Lew like it was coming from the house where the disciples were. When he looked in that direction, he thought he saw a moderately bright light flickering through the windows, but since it was a bright day, it was hard to tell. Then, the noise just ceased.

Everyone was still trying to figure out where the loud roar came from, when the disciples, one by one, came out of the house they were in. As they did, small groups assembled around some of them and were listening to what they said. Lew was too far away to hear them all, and besides, he knew he wouldn't have understood them anyway. That went on for quite a while as groups cycled in and out, seemingly surprised at what the speakers were saying.

As he was watching, one of the disciples, one Lew recognized as one of the more prominent of the group, appeared in a small balcony on the second floor of the house. The clamor in the street outside the building subsided as they looked up at the man in the balcony, who began to address the crowd. As he began to speak, Lew not only heard what he was saying, but to his astonishment, this man was now speaking perfect, unaccented English!

"People of Judea and all who live in Jerusalem, let me explain this to you. Listen carefully to what I am saying"

Lew couldn't believe it!

"These men are not drunk, as you might think. It is only nine in the morning," and he smiled, and some in the crowd chuckled a bit.

"How could they know what he was saying?" Lew wondered.

"No," said the man, continuing. "The prophet Joel spoke of this day.

> *'In the last days, God said, I will pour out My spirit on all people. Your sons and daughters will prophesy, your young men will see visions, and your old men will dream dreams.'"*

Lew was mesmerized! As the man spoke, Lew found himself moving closer to the house, as did others in the crowd.

> *"'I will pour out My spirit on my servant in those days, both men and women. I will show wonders in the heavens above and on the earth below – blood and fire and smoke billowing up. The sun will turn dark, and the moon will turn to blood before the coming of the great and glorious day of the Lord. And everyone who calls on the name of the Lord will be saved!'"*

"Fellow Israelites, listen to this: Jesus of Nazareth was a man accredited by God to you by miracles, wonders and signs, which God did among you through Him, as you yourselves know. This Man was handed over to you by God's deliberate plan and foreknowledge; and you, with the help of wicked men, put Him to death by nailing Him to the cross!

But God raised Him from the dead, freeing Him from the agony of death, because it was impossible for death to keep its hold on Him."

141

"David said about Him:

'*I saw the Lord always before me. Because He is at my right hand, I will not be shaken. Therefore my heart is glad and my tongue rejoices; my body also will rest in hope, because you will not abandon me to the realm of the dead, you will not let your holy One see decay. You have made known to me the paths of life; you will fill me with joy in Your presence.*'"

As he spoke, his voice increased in volume, and he became bolder in what he was saying.

"Fellow Israelites, I can tell you confidently that the patriarch David died and was buried, and his tomb is here to this day. But he was a prophet and knew that God had promised him on oath that He would place one of his descendants on His throne.

Seeing what was to come, he spoke of the resurrection of the Messiah, that He was not abandoned to the realm of the dead, nor did His body see decay. God has raised this Jesus to life, and we are all witnesses of it!"

He was practically shouting as he said that last part and spread out his arms towards the rest of the disciples! He continued, pointing his index finger towards the sky.

"Exalted to the right hand of God, He has received from the Father the promised Holy Spirit and has poured out what you now see and hear."

"For David did not ascend to heaven, and yet he said,

*'The Lord said to my Lord: Sit at my right hand until
I make your enemies a footstool for your feet.'"*

"Therefore let all Israel be assured of this: God has made this Jesus, Whom you crucified, both Lord and Messiah!"

The crowd began to stir. Lewis was impressed with the fervor of this man who was speaking. None of these men were now the dejected men he'd seen after the crucifixion. As a matter of fact, something had caused a monumental change in all of them. There was something confident, without descending into arrogance, about them. It was clear they had each been transformed into different men. He had never seen such a change on such a scale.

As the people in the crowd looked at each other, it was clear they didn't know what to do about what was being said. Someone shouted something to the man on the balcony, and his response made it clear they were asking what to do about this information. So, he spoke again:

"Repent and be baptized, every one of you, in the name of Jesus Christ for the forgiveness of your sins, and you will receive the gift of the Holy Spirit! **This** promise is for you and your children, and for all who are far off – for all whom the Lord our God will call!"

He continued to speak, sometimes answering questions that he either perceived they were thinking, or in a couple of instances, were actually spoken. Finally he said with a pleading forcefulness:

"Save yourselves from this corrupt generation!"

143

With that, the man left the balcony and in a few moments came out of the front door. Lew immediately began making his way towards him. There were several who were talking to, and were waiting to talk to him. These whole conversations were in a language Lew couldn't understand. That was OK, because he wanted to be able to ask his questions.

After several minutes and trying not to appear too impatient, he finally made it to the front of the line. The man spoke to him.

"Yes, brother!"

Lew blinked. English again!

"I have a problem that only you can help me with."

The man put his hand on Lew's shoulder.

"What is your problem, my friend?"

Lew swallowed, then just went right into it.

"I am a traveler from another time – from the 21st century. I don't know how I got here, I can't speak the language, and I don't know how to get back to my own time. The Man who you were with, can He help me?"

"Jesus?" the man asked.

"Yes yes, can He help me?"

"If you believe in the risen Lord, you will receive the eternal life we have all been promised."

Lew frowned. "I understand that message, but what I need is immediate. I need to get home now!"

"Where is your home?" the man frowned.

"The United States, specifically California."

The man frowned again. "I do not know where that is, so I am not sure how to help you."

Lew wanted to kick himself for forgetting there was no United States yet. He had at least accepted that part of his situation.

"I'm sorry," he said, "It is a place that people in this part of the world don't know about yet. But trust me, it is a real place, a beautiful place, and my friends and family are there. I am particularly concerned about what my daughter is thinking now. Where is Jesus?"

The man put his other hand on Lew's other shoulder. "He is not here," he said, "for He has ascended into Heaven and is now with the Father."

Lew's shoulders fell, and he frowned, just short of tearing up. The man saw the agony in Lew's face and said, "Do not be sad, my friend. Here – let me pray for your solution, then I'll see if there's something I can do."

"Whatever," Lew said.

The man bowed his head, and began to pray.

"Father, in the name of the risen Christ, I plead to you for the solution to this man's problem. I can see the agony in his face, and hear the worry in his voice, and I know you are not the God of confusion. When He was here, Your Son told us that with faith we could move mountains. I believe that promise, Father, and ask You in the name of Your Son Jesus Christ to give Your servant Peter an answer for this man. I know You see not only the agony in his face, but in his heart. So, Father, I plead to You to answer his longing. I pray this in the name of Your Son Jesus Christ, Amen."

Lew had actually had his head bowed as well – and that was quite a step for an atheist! When Peter had completed his prayer, he kept his head bowed for another few moments, then looked up into Lew's face.

Lew said, "Well, I understand if you can't help. I just don't know what to do next."

Peter looked at him with the most loving and concerned expression Lew had ever seen.

"I have a suggestion for you, but I cannot tell you exactly what it means."

"Tell me! I need to have some direction!" Lew pleaded.

"This is my suggestion," said Peter. "Go to where it all began."

Go to where it all began? What in the world did that mean?

Peter saw the look in Lew's face, so he placed his hands on Lew's shoulders and again said, more softly this time, "Go to where it all began. That is where you will find your answer."

Just then another of the disciples came over and said something to Peter. Peter said something back to him, then said to Lew, "This is all I have to tell you, my friend. But, we will be praying for your plight. Please, now, if you will excuse me, I have also others to attend to," and with that he patted Lew on the shoulders and turned around to the others waiting for him.

Lew just stood there for a few minutes, not knowing what to do. There were others behind him, and quickly he realized if he didn't move, he might stand out in a way he'd been avoiding. So, he turned and started back down the way he'd come. He walked aimlessly for nearly a half hour, then went to the side of the street and just sat on the ground with his back against one of the stone buildings.

As the day wore on, the crowds began to thin, and Lew eventually found himself sitting alone on the little street. As darkness came, people stopped coming by the street where he was sitting. Suddenly a thought struck him. He'd been in this position before. This reminded him of the street he'd been on that day when he first arrived!

"*Could that be the answer?*" he thought to himself.

146

He jumped up, reoriented himself, then made his way over to the alley where he had stored his clothes. Looking around to make sure no one could see what he was doing, he removed the stone covering the storage area, and reached in and retrieved his clothing. He quickly put on his own clothes, and took the clothing he'd 'borrowed', placed it in the hole, and replaced the stone covering the hole. Then from there, he went to the alley where he'd first arrived and just stood there thinking for a few moments. Finally, he went back over to spot where he'd first 'landed' and sat down and waited. Nothing. He waited more. He looked around for someone to come to his aid. Once, he even looked up into the sky as though the answer was there. Nothing happened. After a couple of hours, dejected and needing sleep again, he decided to just give up. So he laid down and fell fast asleep. Apparently he was stuck here for what would be the rest of his life. With that resignation, he decided he'd just worry about tomorrow when it came, and take it a day at a time.

CHAPTER 29
New Mexico Desert

Second Decade, 2000s

The team was back out in the desert, and everything was ready, the LHC was online, and cockroach #1 was ready in Tent 1. Leonard gave the command, and, after a few moments, got back the standard "Done!" reply. Then he checked outside with Kathy.

"Anything?" he asked over the HT.

"Yes!" came the reply from Kathy. "We are overstocked with cockroaches in Tent 2!"

"Is this a healthy specimen, or do we need to squash it?" Tom asked to Leonard's smirk.

"Oh, I'd like to squash it, OK, but not because there was anything wrong with the specimen itself."

"Gotcha!" Tom said with a chuckle. "OK, ready to send the little guy back to Tent One?"

"Yep!" she said. "Fire when ready Gridley!"

"She's been around you too much," said Leonard.

"I know. I love it!" Tom grinned. "OK, whenever you're ready!"

Leonard typed some commands on the keyboard, and waited, but we didn't get the "Done!" prompt this time. He got an error code instead.

Tom immediately keyed the HT. "Kathy? Everything OK?"

Nothing.

"KATHY?"

For a few heart-stopping moments, silence. Then her voice came over the air, "Nothing out here. What happened?"

Tom breathed a sigh of relief. "I don't know. We're working on it. Did they get *anything* out there?"

"Nope," she said.

"OK, stand by," and he released the transmit switch. "Leonard, what happened?"

"Well, I'm not sure, but I recognize this error code. Remember the first time we tried this, nothing happened, and I discovered we'd branched to a part of the program that had some old code?"

"Yes."

"Well, this is the same error code," he said. "Give me a few minutes and I'll copy the fix from the previous error, since these two areas of code are almost identical."

CHAPTER 30
In the alleyway in Jerusalem

Around 30 A.D.

It was near dawn and Lew was beginning to stir in that nether-land between sleep and awake, and was actually feeling pretty good, as this had been his best night's sleep since he first started watching the disciples.

Suddenly, there was a momentary bright flash, and Lew heard the sound of an alarm clock going off. He immediately jumped up, looked around, rubbed his eyes, then looked around again. He looked over to his left and there, sitting on the edge of his desk in his office, was the alarm clock he'd set to go off, the digits displaying '11:00'. He just stared at it for a second or two, then turned it off. As he did, he heard another sound, apparently some short distance away. "*What is that?*", he asked himself. He then realized it was an alarm klaxon! As he was pondering that realization, he heard an ambulance siren, and as it drew closer to his own building, the klaxon was turned off. Perplexed, his mind in a fog, Lew just sat there and stared at the window.

He'd probably been staring at the window for a good thirty seconds, when there came a knock at the door.

"Dr. Donaldson?" came the voice from the other side of the door.

He just stared at the door.

"Dr. Donaldson, are you in there?" came the voice again.

"Y..Yes," he said. "Just a moment."

He stood and looked around with still no small amount of bewilderment for a second, then went over to the office door, unlocked it, and opened it. On the other side of the door was Lydia's assistant.

"Lydia asked me to check on you in plenty of time for your meeting," she said as she came through the door.

She looked at Lew, then continued. "Your meeting is in less than an hour. What have you been doing? It looks like you slept in your clothes!"

Lew looked down at his clothing.

"Well, I have been, actually. You see, I laid down for a few minutes sleep, but...."

He didn't really know what to say next. She interrupted that thought pattern.

"Well, you might want to change clothes, and straighten up some. You have time, but I don't think you want to show up with the representatives of the Education Department looking all wrinkled and....and what happened to your hair?"

Lew went over to a mirror he kept behind the door and looked at his reflection. His hair was a mess, and he really needed a shave.

"I..I...you won't believe what happened to me...."

"Well," she said, "You have time. Do you have a change of clothes?"

"Yes...yes, I do...." he said trailing off.

She looked at him with a bit of concern. "Are you OK, Dr. Donaldson?"

"Yes....yes, I'm just a bit confused. Wh...What is the date?"

She had a puzzled, but somewhat bemused look on her face as she said, "It's the 10th. You have a meeting in..." and she looked at her watch, "...53 minutes at the restaurant. Lydia will meet you there."

She paused for a few moments, then said, "Are you sure you're OK? Is there anything I can do?"

Lew looked around, then back down at his clothing, then back in the mirror, then back at the young woman standing at the door.

"No, I'll be fine. Thank you, but If you'll excuse me, I need to.....get....ready....I think."

She smiled. "OK, well, I'll be in my office if you need anything."

"Thanks....thank you," he said. She nodded, looked back at him one more time, then shook her head, closed the door, and went back down the hallway. *"Just another day in the life of the absent-minded professor,"* she thought.

Lew just stared at himself in the mirror for a few moments. Then he went over to his desk, woke up the sleeping monitor on his computer, and looked at the date and time. It was less than two hours since he'd gone to sleep on the couch. *"How could this be?"* we wondered.

He looked back at the monitor, noted the time and said out loud, "I've got to get going."

So, he went into the restroom he had in his office, retrieved an extra set of clothes he had hanging on the back of the door, disrobed, took a quick shower, shaved, brushed his hair in place as best he could, and got dressed. Since he had packed before leaving his house, he only needed a few items from his office before departing, so he gathered them together, including the two items he'd retrieved from his classroom, and placed them in his briefcase. His suitcase was already in his vehicle, packed and ready for his trip to the airport to fly out for the week's conference. But, first he had the meeting with Lydia and the Department of Education representatives.

As he was doing all this, his mind kept going over and over what had just happened. As real as everything had seemed, the reality of his office, his bathroom, and especially the water from the shower, and even the clothing he was putting on, led him to what he considered an obvious conclusion: *This had to be the most realistic dream he'd ever had in his life!!*

He didn't really remember the drive over to the restaurant.

CHAPTER 31
Virginia

2001

The next morning, Lew got up in his hotel room in Virginia shortly before eight a.m. to get ready for the conference that started later that morning. He'd arrived late the evening before, but he'd slept enough he felt he could make it through the opening plenary session without nodding off too much. Besides, it didn't start until after lunch. This morning's only event was registration for the conference. He wasn't far from the venue where the conference was to be held, so he had plenty of time to take a shower and go downstairs to get a bite of breakfast before heading over to the conference.

He came back up to his hotel room to retrieve his briefcase and turned on the TV to get a weather update. But, they were not talking about the weather. They were talking about a plane crash. So, he flipped the TV off and prepared to leave for the conference. Checking the contents of his briefcase, he saw the book that had been left in his desk, and once again read the note inside the front cover. He sat down on the edge of the bed, and began to leaf through the book, taking note of the chapter titles. He spent a good fifteen minutes doing this, pausing on one chapter where the book covered the crucifixion of Christ. As he read the words, his mind went back to what he'd convinced himself was a vivid dream, and the images came alive in his mind again. His mind raced, once again, to determine if this had really happened, and had been sitting there several minutes when his watch began to beep, reminding him it was time to leave. He jumped up, put the items he needed in his briefcase, and left for the conference.

When he arrived, he parked his rental, went inside, quickly checked in, and was looking at the schedule for the day when he overheard a group of men to his right talking.

"Do you think they'll cancel the conference?" one of them said.

"My guess is yes. This is just horrible. I can't believe someone would do something like this."

Lew went over to the group.

"Excuse me," he said. "What's this about canceling the conference?"

One of the men answered, "Well, you have heard haven't you?"

"Heard what?" Lew asked.

"The United States has evidently been attacked by terrorists in New York and Washington. They crashed into both of the twin towers in New York, and one of them just collapsed. Then there was another airliner that flew into the Pentagon! There is a report of a third airliner that went down in Pennsylvania that might also have been headed for Washington. The President is on Air Force One, location undisclosed, and there's talk about the FAA grounding the entire airline industry until they figure out what's going on."

Lew was aghast! "Do they know who did it?"

"Speculation is all over the place. The only thing they're sure of is that it was a coordinated attack. I don't see how the conference can continue, since we may all have to drive home now."

Lew found his mouth wide open. He forced it to close for a moment, then said, "I can't believe it!"

"Neither could I, at first," the man said. "But, look!" and he pointed at a TV on the wall.

There, as Lew was watching, suddenly the second tower in New York also fell into a pile of rubble to the gasps and cries of all who were watching.

Lew immediately turned around, went out the door, pulled out his cellular phone, and tried to call his daughter. The circuits were all busy.

He went to the parking garage and retrieved his car. There was no use attending the conference now. That was likely to be canceled. Not sure what else to do, he suddenly thought of his estranged wife, who lived not too far away, so he decided to drive to her house. When he arrived, there were two cars in the driveway. He knocked on the door, and his son answered.

"Dad! Glad to see you! Have you been watching the news?"

"Yes," he said, "and I'm not sure what to do. Is your Mom home?"

"Yes, she is", his son said. "She was sent home when the news began to spread about the attack. Come on in..."

Lew walked in and went into the living room where his wife was intently watching the news.

"Hi, Audrey", he said, and she looked back at him and said "Oh, hi, Lewis. What a mess! I'm guessing they canceled your conference?"

"I think so, but when I realized what had happened, I just left. I guess I'll be heading back to California, but I wanted to come by and see you before leaving. I'm glad you are here as well", he said as he looked over at his son.

"Well, you might have a problem there", she said. "They just grounded all the airlines. Nothing is flying except probably some military aircraft."

"Your kidding!" he said.

"Nope", she answered. "They haven't said how long it will be shut down, but I'm guessing days rather than hours. Do you need a place to stay?"

"No," he answered, "I have all my belongings at the hotel, but if what you're saying is true, I will surely have to drive back home."

"Well, here, come into the kitchen and let me fix us some lunch. It's been a while since we've eaten together."

"Sounds great," Lew said. "Come on, son, let's help out."

As they prepared and ate lunch, they got caught up, then discussed the actions now playing out in New York and Washington. Then the news came on again about the crashes in New York and Washington, and more information about the fourth airliner that crashed in Pennsylvania, plus reiterating the news that the entire airline industry had been grounded. Now there was no question – Lew would have to drive back to California!

Lew stayed most of the afternoon alternating between catching up on each others' lives, and keeping up with the mess that was unfolding live on TV. Finally, he decided it was time for him to go.

"I'll get my belongings together and start for home first thing in the morning, I guess," he said as he walked towards the front door.

His wife and son accompanied him, said their goodbyes, and as he was turning to walk down the sidewalk to his car, his son came behind him.

"Dad," he said, "Are you going to be OK?"

Lew smiled. "Sure, son. I'll be fine. It was good to see you again."

His son frowned a bit, then said, "Are you sure you're OK? You look different."

Lew looked down for a minute, then back up into his son's face. "Well, there have been some things happen lately I have to do some thinking about, but I'll be fine. How about we talk once all this settles down. I'd sure like to keep in touch."

The young man's frown turned to a smile. "I'd like that, too. Call me when you get settled back at home."

"Will do," said Lew, then he put his arms around his son, hugged him tightly, and said, "I love you, son. I'm proud of you!" He released him from the hug, but kept his hands on his son's shoulders, and said, "Take care of yourself. We'll talk when I get back home."

He then walked to his car, looking back one more time, smiled, then got in and drove back toward his hotel.

His son watched as Lew drove away, then went back into his mom's house. She was waiting at the door, having seen the scene that played out on her front lawn.

"Did Dad seem different to you?" he asked.

"Yes, I noticed that. Was he that concerned about the attack?"

"I don't think so," he said. "But, he did say 'some things had happened lately', whatever that means. He promised to call me when he got back home, so maybe I'll find out more then."

"Well," she said, "something's different. I've not seen him hug you like that for a long time."

A small smile came on his face. "Yeah, that was nice," he said. They then went back into the house and watched the news for the rest of the evening.

CHAPTER 32
Virginia

2001

Lew arrived back at his hotel, and began to pack everything up for the long trip back. He called the car rental company to let them know he'd be driving back home and made arrangements to return the car once he arrived back in California.

He started to turn on the TV and see what had happened, but he'd had too many surprises in the last few days, and he just wasn't in the mood. He got ready for bed, and tried to get some sleep, but it just wouldn't come. Finally, he got up, poured himself a glass of cold water, and sat down at the small desk in the hotel room. His suitcase was packed, but on the chair and sitting open. He noticed the book he'd found in his classroom desk, so he reached over to get it. With nothing else to occupy his mind, he began to read...

The next morning, he rose later than he'd planned, having lost several hours of sleep the night before. He put the remainder of his belongings in his suitcase, went downstairs and checked out of his hotel room, retrieved his rental from the parking garage, and headed out of town.

After he had exited the hotel area, he pulled up in the left lane to make a turn at a stoplight and just sat there waiting for the light to change, all the while thinking about all the events of the last several hours, including that wild dream he was still reeling from. As he was waiting, he looked across the street and saw a large building with the door facing the corner towards the street. The sign said it was a Baptist Church. As he sat just staring at it, he heard a horn honking from behind him and he looked up to see the light had changed to green. He made his way through the turn at the intersection and as he was passing the Church he found himself almost absentmindedly turning into the Church's parking lot. He pulled up to a parking place and sat there for a minute. The sign had said 'Welcome', so without really thinking about it, he exited the car and walked up the stairs to the doors.

As he went inside, he noticed the sanctuary was empty, but looking around he couldn't help but be drawn to the sight of the Cross hanging on the wall above the baptistery. He found himself walking towards it. He reached the front of the sanctuary and just stood adjacent to the altar staring at the Cross.

"*Such a sad sight,*" he thought to himself as he remembered the scene from his dream. It had seemed so realistic. But, it had been a dream. Nothing so outlandish could possibly have actually happened – especially to someone like him. He thought of the eyes of Jesus he'd seen that day on those steps, and how that same Man had been beaten within an inch of His life just a few days later, only to be driven to a most horrific death.

As he was thinking about all these things, he felt a tear making its way down his face. A bit surprised at his emotional reaction, he reached in his pocket and retrieved the handkerchief he always carried with him. As he brought it up to his face to wipe the tear, something fell from the handkerchief to the floor. He looked down and saw a small round object. When he reached down to pick it up, his face went white as the blood drained from it, and he suddenly felt light-headed. For, in his right hand was a pristine Roman coin. It was one of the coins Jesus had given him on the street in Jerusalem just days before He was crucified by the Romans, at the behest of the temple priests!

He slowly looked back up at the cross, and then gradually sank to his knees at the altar. As he was kneeling there, he felt a presence come up behind him and realized there was someone else there. Then he heard a voice followed by a gentle hand on his shoulder.

"My name is Collins, and I'm the pastor here. I'd like to pray with you, if that's OK."

Lew looked around at the church pastor, and found an older man with a kind face and an expression of genuine concern.

"Sure, though I'm not sure how to do that, or exactly what to say."

"Well, prayer is one of those things that works differently for each individual. The important thing to know is that no matter what the issue, He is listening. The thing He wants most is to be involved in the conversation. So, how about I start, and you can go from there. You don't even have to speak out loud – He hears you anyway. Would that be OK?"

"Yes, I guess so," said Lew.

"Fine. Here we go"

Brother Collins bowed his head and began to pray.

"Father, in the name of the risen Christ, I pray to You for the solution to this man's problem. I can see the agony in his face, and hear the worry in his voice, and I know You are not the God of confusion. When He was here, Your Son told us that with faith we could move mountains. I believe that promise, Father, and ask You in the name of your Son, Jesus Christ, to provide answers for this man. I know You see not only the agony in his face as I do, but in his heart as well. So, Father, I plead to You to answer his longing. I pray this in the name of our Savior, the risen Christ, Amen."

As Brother Collins finished his prayer, Lew was aghast. This was almost the exact prayer Peter had prayed that day in Jerusalem when Lew was trying to get back home. At that realization, Lew immediately began to cry. All his life he'd denied even the possibility of an all-supreme Being, and yet here he was, in a church of all places, experiencing the most profound case of deja-vu in history! Suddenly, he found himself talking.

"God – I have never really believed You existed. But I now find I have no choice. I don't really know what to do."

He paused for a minute before continuing.

"But, I've been in a situation like this before, and I suppose my best bet is to rely on the one You sent me today. Please show me what to do. I need to understand."

Not knowing what else to say, he simply said, "Thanks".

He looked up to the Pastor and simply said, "What now?"

Brother Collins just smiled and said, "That is the question of all of life, now isn't it? At some time, at some place in life, everyone asks what life is all about. Those who decide to honestly seek the truth will eventually be forced to face who God is, and what to do with what they find – and they will have a decision to make. If their decision is the correct one, and the honest one, they'll always have that time and place to keep reminding them. Some of us are forced to keep revisiting that point time and time again."

Lew had no choice but to laugh. Brother Collins patted him on the shoulder and said, "I won't pretend to have all the answers to all of life's questions, but I can point you in the direction where you can find answers. Is that OK with you?"

162

Lew nodded and said, "Yes – at this point I'm ready for anything."

Brother Collins then said, "Good, then I'd like to introduce you to the Man who changed my life – Jesus Christ."

Lew teared up again, but didn't say what he wanted to say – "*Yeah, I've already met Him – and He winked at me!*" Instead, he simply listened as Brother Collins presented the message of Salvation to him.

CHAPTER 33
September

2001

All those hours on the road back to the west coast gave Lew plenty of time to think. He stopped to spend the night in a hotel somewhere outside St. Louis. As he sat on the end of the bed just staring out the window, the words of Peter came back to him.

"Repent and be baptized, every one of you, in the name of Jesus Christ for the forgiveness of your sins, and you will receive the gift of the Holy Spirit!"

Lew Donaldson bowed his head and softly said, "OK, Lord. I get it. I still don't know exactly what You want me to do, but if You'll let me know, I'll do it. I don't know why You chose me, but I'll follow You, and do whatever You tell me to do. *I saw You.* I know that it is You who has saved me."

Suddenly, he remembered the book he'd brought with him on the trip, and went over to the suitcase and retrieved it. For the next several hours, he began to devour every chapter, trying to get a deeper understanding. When he turned the last page, he found a folded tract innocuously enough named 'The Roman Road', and began to read.

Dawn came, and as the sun rose into the sky, he knew exactly what to do. He got up, went over to the nightstand, fished a card out of his pocket, lifted the telephone handset and dialed it.

"Hello...Brother Collins? Do you have a few minutes?"

The voice on the other end of the line said, "Yes, Lew. I've been expecting your call."

"Thanks," said Lew. "I think this is my time and place, and I wanted you to be the first to know."

After talking to and praying with the pastor on the phone, Lew, tears in his eyes, said goodbye to Brother Collins, and decided to make another call. He dialed the number, the phone rang, and the voice on the other end said "Hello".

"Audrey?" asked Lew.

"Yes..." she said somewhat apprehensively.

Lew smiled as he said, "I have something to tell you."

CHAPTER 34

2001

By the time Lew arrived back home, he had completely changed the direction of his life. No longer was he the atheist history professor he'd spent his life becoming. All those hours on the road, especially the conversations he'd had with the very Man he'd seen on that cross wearing that crown, left him with no choice but to follow Him.

The following Monday morning, as Lew was in his office preparing his class notes for the week, he received a call from Lydia's secretary asking him if he had a few minutes to come by her office. A few minutes later, Lew entered Lydia's office.

"Good morning, Lew," she said. "How was your trip?"

"Well, eventful would be an understatement," he said, "but the drive back gave me plenty of time of think about several things. But, I made it back OK, so thanks for asking. What did you want to talk about this morning?"

Lydia paused, placed her clasped hands on the desk in front of her and said, "I heard back from the grant chairman yesterday, and based on the events going on in the country right now, they are freezing all grant money until they know what the situation is going to be. They're afraid funds are going to be reallocated, and I'm inclined to believe them."

Lew sat back in his chair for a moment, then calmly said, "I'm inclined to agree with them, as well. That was one of the conclusions I came to on the way back, along with some personal decisions."

"Really," Lydia said, more of a statement than an answer. "So, this news is not surprising to you?"

"Not really," he said. "I'm struggling now with these personal issues as well, so this may be as helpful as it is disappointing. I suppose I'm fine with that outcome, at least for the time being."

Lydia sat back. Her face softened, and she allowed a small sympathetic smile as she said, "I know you're disappointed, but you may be right. With events unfolding so fast, I believe things are going to change more than we know."

"You're right!" said Lew, while at the same time thinking, without saying, "*You have no idea!*"

They ended the meeting cordially, and Lew went on to his class. There was a palatable change in the mood in his class, not the least of which was Lew's. He still had some decisions to make.

Over the next couple of weeks, Lew had several conversations with Audrey, not only about his conversion, but about the direction of his life, and it quickly became apparent there might be a change in their relationship as well. As they talked, sometimes more than once a day, even over the phone, they could both tell the other was rethinking their separation.

Finally, late one evening, after spending the day in prayer (something that was still entirely new to Lew!), he picked up the phone.

"Audrey?" he asked when she answered the call.

"Yes, Lew?"

"How do you feel about my coming and spend a few days. The Thanksgiving break is coming up, and I'll have some time off. Would you be be OK with that?"

Audrey smiled, and Lew could actually hear it in her voice as she replied, "That would be wonderful! Let me know when you're coming in, and I'll pick you up at the airport."

Now it was time for Lew to smile. "Sounds great! Let me put it together, and I'll let you know."

When they hung up, Lew made one more call.

"Hi, Brother Collins. Do you have a few minutes?"

A few weeks later, Lew met Audrey at the airport. They were both apprehensive about the weekend, but it was a happy meeting, as both realized their relationship might possibly change for the better. Their separation had not been acrimonious, and as it had turned out, not even planned, but it was definitely something Audrey had regretted and now, so had Lew.

When they reached her home, they sat at the dinner table together over coffee and had a frank discussion about the nature of their marriage. As both realized they now wanted the same thing, the discussion morphed into what to do about Lew's career.

"Well," began Lew finally, "with the loss of funding on my research, and with the state of the world right now, I think it may be time for me to make a change. How would you feel about our moving back together?"

"I'd like that!" said Audrey. "Where were you thinking about living?"

"Well," said Lew, sneaking a smile on his face, "how about here?"

As he looked at Audrey, he saw her eyes tear up. She looked down at her hands for an instant, then said, "I'd like that very much!"

Lew reached over and laid his hands on hers.

"Well, it's decided, then."

Audrey looked up and said, "But what about Caltech?"

"Caltech may be looking for a new professor," said Lew. "I have enough in my savings and investments to decide what to do next, so how about we both take that time to make a good decision – for the both of us."

Audrey clasped her hands around Lew's, and the decision was made.

That Saturday afternoon, Lew called the Dean at Caltech and told him he needed to take a sabbatical, and that he had contacted a fellow professor to cover his classes for the next couple of weeks. When the Dean asked if Lew was OK, Lew replied, "Yes, I'm fine. I just have some personal things to sort out."

The Dean wished him well, and Lew promised to call him in a few days, and they ended the call. Now Lew was wondering just what the content of that call might be. Right now, he really had no idea. He did, though, know one place he would seek the answers.

Brother Collins was in his office when Lew came knocking at the door.

"Hi, Lew," he said. "How are you doing?"

"Well," said Lew, "I'm doing as well as can be expected for someone who just turned his life upside down."

Brother Collins smiled. "I suspect you might find that you've actually turned your life right-side up, but that's something for you to discover. Are there ways I can help?"

169

"I'm sure there are," said Lew as they both sat down. "As you know I'm new to this 'prayer' thing, but from what I've read, and actually experienced, that appears to be a source I had never really considered before. Can you give me some hints?"

Brother Collins chuckled, and said, "I can give you some personal experience, but here are a couple of things to keep in mind. When you're talking to God, you're talking to the Creator of the universe, so there's always an air of respect you have to keep in mind. But, you're talking to Him through His Son, who is not only the one responsible for your salvation, but He is the closest friend you'll ever have. So, I always just talk frankly about my issues as I would to any close friend. I let Him know my problems, but I'm also constantly thanking Him for things He's already revealed, and for His guidance and protection."

"As I told you on the phone earlier, Audrey and I have decided to move back in together, and we're going to live here."

"That's wonderful!" said Brother Collins with a big smile on his face. "Where, if you don't mind my asking, will you be attending church?"

Lew smiled. "I was thinking about a Church I know of where a friend of mine is the Pastor. I believe you know him very well. You probably saw him last in your mirror this morning…."

That brought a big smile and laugh to both of them.

"We'd be honored to have you here," said Brother Collins. "At least that way I can keep an eye on the only atheist I know well."

"Former atheist," said Lew. "Former atheist! Newly reconciled with his wife, as well!"

"As the song says, '*There is no secret what God can do*'," said Brother Collins. "I don't know why we're surprised when He actually does stuff!"

"I know," said Lew. "I'm just beginning to figure that out. On that subject, I'm facing some rather radical life changes. Would you mind praying with me about the decisions we have to make in the next few days? I'm guessing your communications with God are a bit clearer than mine."

"I'd be glad to," said Brother Collins, "but don't get the idea He hears me better than He hears you. I would suspect He's been longing to hear from you your entire life. But, let's go to Him together."

For the next several minutes both Lew and Brother Collins reached out to the only One who knew all the answers, both looking for some of that clarity that only comes when you honestly ask Him.

CHAPTER 35

2002

Over the next couple of weeks, Lew had serious conversations with Audrey, with Brother Collins, and spent much time in this new thing to him called 'prayer', trying to look for some of that clarity Brother Collins had spoken of. During of all this, he and Audrey attended the Sunday services at the Church. By the middle of the second week, Lew had come to at least one conclusion: He no longer saw himself as a returning professor of history at Caltech. So, he called the Dean and informed him he wouldn't be coming back. To say the Dean was surprised was a bit of an understatement, but when Lew explained his life situation, the Dean let it go, and they parted friends. The Dean even said he'd have Lew's personal effects from his office packed and sent to his new address. Lew promised to come by and see him when he returned to move out of his apartment near the university.

The hard part, though, was his call to his daughter.

"Hi Dad," she said when she answered the phone. "What's going on?"

"I have some news," said Lew. "I have decided to leave Caltech and move back with your mother."

There was a pause on the other end of the phone.

"You're leaving California?" she asked.

"Yes," he said, "and so far the hardest part has been knowing I'll be leaving you there."

"I....I....understand." she said. "So, this is a good news/bad news call?" and she let out a small chuckle.

"Well," he said, "it's mostly good news. First, of course, your mother and I have decided to resume our marriage, which as you know, has been in a state of limbo for a while. The best part of this news, though – and hang on to your hat – is I've become a believer in Jesus Christ."

"Wow! Just, wow!" she exclaimed. "After all the lectures you gave me about how deluded these Christians were, and now you *are* one? Man, Dad, blow me over with a feather. What does Mom think about all this?"

"That's the funny part," said Lew. "She is ecstatic about it! Turns out she had been praying about this very thing. Kinda puts a positive spin on this religion thing, don't you think?"

She chuckled a little again, and said, "Well, I'm glad you two are finally getting back together, of course. And as for the 'religion' thing, as you called it, I'm a bit shocked. Are you sure about all this?"

"More than sure," he said. "I'm positive about it all. The weird thing is that quitting my teaching position was much easier than I would have ever thought. But, what I really want to know is how you feel about all this?"

"I guess I feel OK about it," she said, "but I'm really going to miss our Sunday meals. But, as always, I want you and Mom to be happy."

"That's what we're working toward," he said. "It seems to be the right direction. Listen, I have to come back to California to close out some things and get all my belongings moved. When I do, let's get together and spend some time over dinner and we'll go from there."

"Yes, I'd like that," she said. "If you and Mom are happy, I'll be good."

"I'm glad to hear that!" said Lew. "Listen, I love you very much, so let's both hang on to that, and we'll catch up when I come to town."

Lew could almost hear the smile over the phone. "I love you, too, and tell Mom the same. We'll talk when you come to town."

They hung up, and Lew realized there was much to do, including figuring out what he was going to do with the rest of his life.

After the call, he told Audrey about the conversation, relieved that it had gone well.

"I need to call her, too," she replied. "I talked to her a little over a week ago, but much has happened since then, and Mom needs to take her temperature!"

They both laughed.

"That's a great idea," said Lew, "and speaking of great ideas, here's one. What do you say about a small vacation – just the two of us?"

"Hmmm…" said Audrey, "I think that's just the ticket. Mountains or beach?"

"Mountains," said Lew. "I need to get a fresh perspective on the world."

"Mountains it is!" she replied. "I know just the place. Are you OK with me booking it?"

"Yes. Yes I am!" Lew said as he smiled. "You know the area better than I do, so set it up and let me know when we leave."

Audrey had picked a great cabin for the week, and as Lew looked out at the magnificent view across the Appalachians, suddenly the world seemed different. For him, of course, it was. It was early in the morning as he sat on the balcony, Bible in hand, and a nice hot cup of coffee, contemplating what direction he wanted to go. An early riser for most of his life, Lew had done this the last couple of mornings as Audrey, who was the late sleeper of the pair, slept in. Lew liked this time his first morning here, and he had decided that waking early and spending his time in study and contemplating his life might just be how he wanted to spend every morning.

Since his conversion from atheism to full-blown Christianity, Lew was basically starting over – or at least that's how he saw it. He was studying the book of Matthew, following the journey Jesus took during his three-year ministry. and as he did, thoughts of those exact places came back into his memory. *"Had that been real, or was it just a hyper-realistic dream?"*, he wondered. There were times when he was convinced it was real, and times when he was just as convinced it was all a dream, or a really deep hallucination. But, then, that Roman coin he kept hidden in his wallet was hard to explain. He wasn't sure he'd ever really know, but suddenly he had a longing to find out. How was he going to do that?

Audrey came through the door, coffee in hand.

"Mornin' sunshine!" said Lew.

"G'mornin'," she replied.

"How'd you sleep?" he asked.

"Like a rock!" she said with a still-sleepy smile. "Best rest I've had in years!"

"Yeah, me, too." said Lew. "Wanna stay here forever?"

"Yep!" she said, as she sat down. "Whatcha doin'?"

Lew knew he couldn't say exactly what he was thinking, because he didn't want her to think he was insane, so he just said "Just doing some studying. I'm reading about all the places Jesus went when He was here. Some of these places I've heard of...."

Audrey smiled. "You don't know how glad, and if I'm honest, surprised I am that you're really getting into this. Even when I prayed for you all those years, I never expected this."

"How do you think I feel?" he asked. "This was the absolute last thing I expected, too! But, here we are, and I have a whole new view of reality." Again, he couldn't tell her about all of his 'reality', because he still wasn't sure how it all happened.

"Well, this is most definitely an answer to my prayers. Will you pinch me so I'll know," she said as she chuckled.

He did.

"Ouch!" she exclaimed. "I was just kidding! But, thanks, I guess. It's definitely real!"

They both had a good laugh, and then spent the next few minutes just in awe of the magnificent view.

A few days later, it finally was their last night in the mountains, and they decided instead of eating at one of the many local restaurants, they would just spend their last evening at the cabin. Audrey prepared an excellent meal, and when they sat down to eat, Lew said, "Before we eat, is it OK if we pray?"

Tears came to Audrey's eyes as she said, "That'd be perfect!"

They both bowed their heads, and Lew began. "Lord, I'm still not sure how all this works, but I just want to let You know I'm trying to figure it all out. Thanks for letting Audrey and me get back together, and I guess thanks as well for the new-found direction in life, wherever that ends up being. Help us both to find out where You want us to go with all this, and I'll try to listen for Your direction. As You know, I'm not very practiced in this yet, so cut me some slack if I don't get it right the first time. We're thankful You allowed us to have this time together, and for this great meal Audrey prepared. Please keep us safe as we travel home tomorrow. Amen."

As he looked up, Audrey had a wide smile on her face.

"What?" he asked.

"Just never thought I'd see you do this," she said.

"Yeah, it's the last thing I expected, too," he said with a bit of a smirk. "But - let's eat!"

And with that they began their meal. As they were doing so, there was a lull in the conversation, and Audrey noticed Lew seemed to have something on his mind.

"You OK over there?" she asked. "Looks like you're working on something."

"Well," he began, "as I was saying that prayer, I caught myself saying 'new found direction, wherever that ends up being'."

"OK....," she said.

Lew continued, "I just had a thought about seeing where this all actually began."

"What do you mean 'where this all began'," she asked.

Suddenly, the conversation with Peter came back into his head, as those were the same words Peter had said when Lew was looking for answers. Then, it dawned on him.

"What do you think about a trip to Israel?" he asked.

"Overseas?" she asked. "That's a pretty big trip!"

"I know," said Lew as he was quickly working it all out in his head. "But, there's still plenty left in our savings, so we can afford the trip, and I really need to get my head around this new reality

I'm dealing with. Call it a 'working vacation', but I'd like to at least see some of the things the Bible talks about."

Audrey contemplated that for a moment, then realized that when Lew had said 'direction', maybe that's what they both were looking for. Then a smile came on her face.

"That actually sounds like a great idea!" she exclaimed. "How soon do you want to leave?"

"Well," he said, "I don't know how things work over there. Is there someone we can call – maybe we can find a tour guide or something."

"Tell you what," she said. "As soon as we get back home, I'll start making some calls and see what the deal is for people who just want to visit some of the Holy Land sites."

"Great!" Lew said. "If you'll look into the tour aspects, I'll talk to a travel agent and see what we can put together."

CHAPTER 36

2002

Six weeks later, they were packing to go. The biggest hurdle was getting Audrey's passport updated, as it had been a while since she'd been overseas, but after jumping through a few hoops, the passport issue was taken care of. They also had to find a tour guide. There were some organizations in the U.S. who conducted tours of the Holy Land, but those all had waiting lists that were fairly long (one even had at least a two-year lead time). So, Lew worked some of his many contacts. He was able to get in contact with a tour company in Israel that one of his friends said was very reputable, and after some phone calls and a few email exchanges, they were all set.

Late one Friday night, Lew and Audrey showed up at the airport, boarded a flight, and a couple of layovers later they arrived in Tel Aviv. From there they hired a driver to take them to their hotel in Jerusalem, where they tried to sleep off the jet lag. By Monday morning, they were ready to go. About ten a.m. local time, the phone rang, and it was their tour guide calling from the lobby. A few minutes later, itinerary in hand, Lew was shaking hands with him.

"Nice to meet you. My name, as you probably already know, is Lew Donaldson, and this is my wife Audrey."

"A pleasure," said the tour guide. "My name is Daniel Weiss, and I will be your personal guide to all the sites you wish to visit."

He then shook hands with Audrey, and said, "And it is nice to make your acquaintance, Audrey."

"Likewise," said Audrey. "We're very much looking forward to the experience."

Daniel motioned to the door, and said, "We have a nice four passenger vehicle, I think you call them 'SUV's', waiting just outside, so if you are ready, I feel it would be a good idea to go over your itinerary. There is a small open air cafe just down the road, and the weather is pleasant today. Does that meet with your approval?"

Lew and Audrey looked at each other and Lew said, "That sounds great."

"Fine," said Daniel. "This way, then, and we will get started."

As they were walking out of the hotel, Lew said, "You seem to have a good working knowledge of English. Are you originally from here?"

"Yes," said Daniel. "My grandparents immigrated here from England after they had escaped Poland during the war. However, I require a working knowledge of many languages as a result of my work."

"So, you've been doing this for a while?"

"Most of my adult life," said Daniel. "A friend of my parents began doing these tours many years ago, and I began working with him in my teens."

"How many languages do you know?" asked Audrey.

"Eight, some just enough to have basic conversations without difficulty, but there are others where I have more fluency."

"That's amazing! I have enough difficulty with english," she said with a chuckle.

"As you know, there are many languages spoken in this region," Daniel said, "so most people here know at least one other language enough to be understood."

They boarded the SUV and arrived a few minutes later at the cafe. They each decided on a cup of coffee, and Daniel began going over the details of their itinerary.

"These are the sites you had chosen that you were most interested in when you talked to our representative," said Daniel as he reviewed the list of sites with them. "You may also choose other sites, so long as we are conscious of any security issues."

"How will we know about what locations might pose a risk," asked Audrey.

"That is my job," said Daniel. "You simply tell me what you would like to see, and if there are concerns, we will discuss them at that time."

"I am primarily interested in Jerusalem," said Lew, "so the sites on this list are a great starting place. There is one other place I'm interested in. I would also like to see the area where the Apostles were on the Sunday of Pentecost. Is that possible?"

"Yes, I have been to there many times," said Daniel. "Where would you like to begin?"

Lew looked at Audrey, and asked, "Any place you'd like to start?"

"I would like to see the crucifixion site first, if that's OK," she said.

Lew nodded as he looked back towards Daniel.

"Sounds good to me," he said. "Can we start with the crucifixion site, then maybe the *Via Dolorosa*?"

Daniel smiled. "You tourists are all alike. Yes, these will be fine."

"Great," said Lew. "We can decide the rest after these two."

Lew had great hopes for the tour. He was still in denial about actually having been here before, and though the experience (real or imagined) had precipitated the greatest change in his life, he still wondered if it had actually happened. So, when they reached the crucifixion site, he carefully examined every little detail.

As Daniel explained the significance of the features, and as he listened to the presentation given by the people on site, he couldn't see anything that he remembered. Of course, as a historian, Lew knew that geological features changed over time, and in many cases, original sites that existed centuries ago were covered and buried by changes brought forth both by natural processes and by human intervention. Sometimes it didn't take centuries.

However, in this case, Lew couldn't even find a reference as to where he might had been in his previous 'excursion'. The fact that, over the years, men had constructed the venues to both honor and, in some cases, obscure some of these sites didn't help Lew as he tried to orient himself.

Audrey, of course, was just soaking up all the history, because she had no idea about the thoughts crashing around in Lew's head. Lew had resigned himself to the fact she would never know, because how in the world could he explain it? He was sure no one would ever really know. Well, almost no one. He was becoming more and more aware of the idea that there was Someone who had already known about it, and that Someone had winked at him one day. Whether it was in a dream, or a physical reality was still up for grabs.

Next they went to the *Via Dolorosa*, the path that presumably Christ had taken from His trial and sentencing to the place where

He would be crucified. They stopped along the way at a small cafe, and Lew treated them all to a quick bite to eat. As they arrived at the *Via Dolorosa*, Lew was surprised.

"Wait a minute," he said to Daniel as they were about to enter. "I didn't realize this was under ground!"

"Yes," said Daniel, "over the years the building, rebuilding, construction, and renewal of the city would have buried this path, and there was a great desire to preserve it as much as possible. So, eventually, the city above was simply built around it!"

"Are you saying this is the actual route Jesus took on the way to Calvary?" Audrey asked.

Daniel paused for a moment, then said, "I cannot say this is all the actual path. As you may know, the city was destroyed in the first century, and taken over by enemies of the Jewish people. It was some time later that the restoration was begun, and of course, there was much that had to be reconstructed. There are some points on this path that were original to that day, but since no one is alive who was actually there, it was restored as much as it could be, given the conditions."

As they walked the underground route, some of which went through connection doorways and pathways, Audrey was once again soaking in all that she saw, while Lew was still trying to find something that would indicate he had been there before.

Daniel was right. It was obvious that much had changed from what would have been there two millennia ago, and to Lew's dismay, he now presumed much of this had been constructed as example, rather that fact. Some of it probably was fact, but in his previous excursion, Lew had only been on a small part of this trail, and it was possible that small part had been obscured over the centuries.

It was getting late in the afternoon, so they decided to stop for the day. Lew and Audrey were still suffering from a bit of jet lag, and all the walking they'd done sure didn't help matters. Daniel dropped them off at their hotel and they decided what time to resume the following day. Tired, they both wanted to spend an hour or so in their hotel room to decompress, then have the concierge recommend a restaurant for dinner.

As Lew lounged on the sofa, he went through the day's journey in his mind. While he had only been here one day, he was a bit disappointed he'd recognized nothing from his previous experience here. '*Was it real?*", he kept asking himself, '*or was that just a really vivid dream?*'. This was one of the primary questions Lew had hoped to answer on this trip.

However, the sites he'd seen, and the descriptions of Christ's journey to where the Romans would crucify Him did have an effect on him. While he was in these thoughts, he looked over at Audrey and saw she was also deep in thought.

"Tell me what you're thinking," Lew said.

Audrey turned towards him in her chair.

"I guess when you see something like this," she began, "it just reminds you how real this is. I mean, it's one thing to read about it and talk about it, but it's something completely different when you walk in His steps, and see the place where He was so brutally murdered. It makes me ashamed of how caviler we sometimes are about what He did for us on the Cross."

'*How real this is*', Lew thought. How he wished she could read his thoughts about that. She was right, though. Even if he couldn't place himself here, there was still that reality that would jump out at you once you were here.

"I know what you mean," he said. "I spent my life denying this happened, or at least that it meant what I now believe it meant. I'm still not sure how to process all this. But, I'm working on it."

"I know," she said. "I could see you working on it all day!"

"*If she only knew,*" Lew thought.

An hour or so later, they went to a nearby restaurant recommended by the hotel concierge where they tried the local cuisine. Some of it they liked, some not, but they both had a good meal, and returned to the hotel room early enough try to finish heading off the remaining jet lag.

CHAPTER 37

2002

After a restful night, they met Daniel the next morning for the day's excursion. Daniel drove them to the city of Nazareth to visit the sites of Jesus' boyhood. Jesus had grown up there, and Audrey was especially excited to see the place where He lived with His parents. The sites maintained there were very informative, and they could both imagine a young Jesus with His father learning the carpentry trade. The tour guides there stressed that Nazareth was likely a small, poor village, and demonstrated that idea by explaining how life would have been in the first century.

Next, Daniel drove them to Bethlehem, the birthplace of Christ. On the way he explained that, like many of the tour's stops, the site of Jesus' birth was somewhat in dispute, but even if the chosen site was not the exact birthplace, one could still imagine the scene on that first Christmas morning two thousand years ago.

When they arrived, both Lew and Audrey began to feel how special this place was. As they had now come to believe, the Savior of the world, God in human form, was born in this place. While the exact location might be in dispute, just being in the same place where He had come into the world gave them a sense of reverence.

On the way back, Daniel noticed a change in the demeanor of both his passengers.

"I sense you both are having some deep thoughts about where we just visited," he said. "That is natural, I suppose. I have seen that many times with others I have carried on my tour. But, if you do not mind me saying so, you seem especially moved, Mr. Donaldson."

Lew replied, "I guess so. You see, just a few months ago, I was an atheist. I had absolutely no belief that there had been a heavenly visitor to earth, because I didn't believe there was a God."

That was a new one for Daniel.

"My, that is quite a turn around," he said. "If you do not mind my asking, what changed your mind?"

"I guess you could say I had an encounter I couldn't explain away," Lew said. "I was on a trip back home from a conference that had been canceled because the 9-11 attacks and had a lot of time to think. In a motel room on the way home, I started reading a book a student of mine had given me and, well, events just came together. On my knees that night, I sought the truth, and God was gracious enough to reveal it to me. So, I'm still on a voyage of discovery, I guess you could say."

Daniel thought about that for a moment, then said, "That must have been quite a revelation. I can say for certain I have never been with someone who had such a reversal of belief."

Lew smiled. "Well, I guess once you're ready to find out the truth, and you're willing to go wherever it takes you, God will visit you at a time and a place of His choosing, and that's when miracles happen."

After that exchange, they were all lost in their thoughts for the trip back to Jerusalem. Lew had decided to call it a day, as he wanted to get back to his hotel and consider the things he'd seen and heard. Plus, he wanted to spend some time in his Bible reading about these places they had just visited. Audrey had agreed, because she also wanted to contemplate the day's events.

They agreed to meet again the next morning and see the Upper Room site where Jesus is supposed to have met with His disciples before his arrest. Their next stop would then be the Garden at the Mount of Olives where He had spent His last night.

It was late when Lew and Audrey finally went to bed, and they stayed awake a while longer and exchanged their thoughts on what they'd seen so far.

As he turned over to go to sleep, Lew felt a bit guilty about not telling the full story when Daniel had asked earlier that day, but the real reason for his questioning his own life choices was still just too incredible to tell anyone. Again, he was now even more certain he'd never be able to tell anyone – at least not on this planet!

When the morning came, Audrey and Lew readied themselves for the day's excursion. While there had been plenty of time for sleep, Lew had trouble going to sleep the night before, as he'd had many thoughts pinging around in his head, not only of what they'd seen, but of what they would see the next day. He wondered if he would recognize anything from the Upper Room site, since he'd read that this was not only the place where Jesus and His disciples had their final meal, but it was believed to also be the place where the Pentecost took place some weeks later. Lew knew a thing or two about that, since he'd been there at the time….*or had he*? That was the real question for today.

They met Daniel in front of the hotel at the appointed time, and began the short trip to the Upper Room site. When they arrived, this was not exactly the venue Lew remembered. In his previous encounter, there had been a courtyard here capable of holding the thousands of people that had gathered when the loud rushing sound drew them into the area. Lew could almost hear it again, but when he realized there was actually an aircraft high overhead, it was almost déjà vu!

As it was, there was barely room for a few dozen people with all the structures surrounding the site. As he stood there looking at the building purported to be the Upper Room, there were both some feelings of familiarity, and feelings of unfamiliarity, and that just confused Lew even more.

Daniel accompanied them to the upstairs room, which was essentially an empty room, but Lew could imagine a table large enough to seat the thirteen participants at the Last Supper, as well as room for servers and other attendants to mill about. While Lew had not gone this far in his original episode, he still had feelings of humbleness when he realized this might be the actual place that Christ had been on his last night before his arrest, interrogation, and the beatings that followed.

Audrey, as it turns out, had similar feelings, and as they both stood together, she reached out and held his hand as they just looked around the room and imagined what it must have been like.

Finally, ready to leave, Daniel accompanied them back down to the street below and they entered the SUV, and circled around to the road that led to the Mount of Olives. When they arrived, the on-site guides led them around the Mount, and explained how that last night might have occurred. When they were taken to the Garden area of the Mount, the guide showed them one of the possible places where Jesus would have knelt to pray. As she talked, Lew looked around and tried to imagine the disciples a short distance away struggling, and failing, to stay awake while Jesus poured out His soul to the Father, being in such a state of stress that blood vessels ruptured and mixed themselves with the accompanying perspiration. He literally 'sweat drops of blood', such was his stress level.

On each of these stops, from the *Via Dolorosa*, to the crucifixion site, the Upper room, and now the Garden, Lew was more and more becoming aware of the reality of the events described in the Bible, and he realized that one didn't need a 'vivid dream' or an actual 'visit' back in time to conclude that the momentous events described in the Bible had an actual ring of reality.

But — he couldn't shake the feeling that he might have actually been here. That was just a feeling, though, as his mind still couldn't accept anything close to reality.

As they were leaving the Garden site, Lew asked Audrey what she wanted to do about lunch.

"I've seen some street food vendors at various sites along the way," she said. "What do you think about trying one of those."

"Sounds like a great idea," he said. Then he tapped Daniel on the shoulder and asked, "What do you think, Daniel. Can we find an outdoor place to grab a meal for lunch?"

"Of course," said Daniel. "I know a place. It is an outdoor area just a short distance from here. I think you will like it."

Lew and Audrey exchanged glances, and Lew said, "Sounds great! Let's go there and we'll all get something to eat, and maybe look around some."

With that, Daniel left the Garden site, and a short time later they pulled up to an area beside a building where, just beyond, Lew could see several people milling about. They exited the SUV and walked up to the area where there were several small merchants set up, at least three of which were selling food.

"Pick a place, Daniel, and I'll get us all something to eat," he said.

Daniel made a beeline to one of the vendors, obvious that he'd eaten here before, and ordered his selection in the local language. *'That's oddly familiar'*, thought Lew as he stepped up and asked if the man understood english. He nodded and asked what they would like. He and Audrey made their selection, then went over to an area where some picnic tables had been set up.

When they finished their meal. Audrey rose and said, "If you two don't mind, I want to look around a bit. I noticed a man selling some clothing and fabric on the other side of this food place, and I want to look through some of what he has."

"Fine with me," said Lew. "I can mill about the place as well. Whenever you're finished, we'll meet back here at the table."

Daniel, still munching on the last bites of his lunch just nodded and said, "I will be right here. I may get one of the other delights this vendor has."

With that Audrey left and went towards the vendors on her right. Lew stood and looked around for a second, and started ambling his way towards the other side of the market area. Daniel got up and went over to the food vendor's booth, and after surveying the goods, selected his favorite pastry – a mutabak (he preferred the cheese) and returned to his seat at the picnic table.

Daniel was in a position where he could see the entire market area, so he felt comfortable letting his charges ramble about, knowing if they needed assistance, he could get to them easily. He watched Audrey as she made her way to the tables containing clothing and fabrics where she started sorting through the wares the man had for sale.

Lew was really just killing time, as he had nothing he was specifically looking for, so he wandered from table to table, and booth to to booth just seeing what there was on display.

Daniel was finishing his dessert and the drink he had refilled when he bought it. This went on for several minutes, so he just sat enjoying the fine afternoon.

Lew had made his way to one end of the market area, and turned around and started making his way back. He hadn't found anything that interested him, so he decided to return to the table where Daniel was seated to await Audrey.

As he did, he noticed something out of the corner of his eye. It was a table set up near the edge of the market opposite from the direction he'd been wandering. There was something familiar about it, so he stopped and started walking towards the vendor set up there. Suddenly he stopped.

"I've been here before!"

CHAPTER 38

2002

As Lew stood there, visions of his previous trip rushed back into his memory. It was as if he'd been transported right back to this same space two thousand years before. For there, on the end of the table, just like before, were several sandals for sale! Then he turned and looked to his left and saw a narrow passageway opposite the vendor. Then, he looked back at the vendor, and just to the right of the table and behind it was another passage that opened up into the market area.

"*It can't be!*", he thought. Turning back towards the first passage, he mumbled to himself, "I came in there, then walked over to the table...", and he turned back towards the vendor, "...then when I'd bought the sandals, I left through that street and put them on!

Lew couldn't believe it! Of all the sights they'd viewed, and all the possible places he might have recognized, it was this place that brought it all back in his memory. Almost subconsciously, he started over towards the table where the sandals were on display.

When he arrived at the table, he started sorting through the sandals, and found a pair not much unlike the ones he'd purchased before. The vendor, noticing him, came over and stood before him.

"*Eich ephshar la-azor l'kha?*", asked the vendor. Lew stood there stunned for a moment, then as if it were scripted, he held out the sandals, then, with his fingers, rubbed them together with the universal signal for '*How much?*'

"*Sh' sheemsh qualeem,*" said the vendor. Lew, of course, still had no idea what he'd said, so he pulled out his wallet, selected a $20 bill, and offered it to the vendor. This time the vendor simply took the money, went over to a small metal cash box, opened it, dropped the bill into it, selected some other bills, and returned and gave it to Lew as his change. Lew paused for a moment, then smiled, put his hands to his chest, and bowed slightly. The vendor smiled, and Lew turned and went over to the passage beside the vendor, where he sat down, removed his shoes and socks, and put the sandals on.

As he sat there and looked out over the marketplace, just like he'd done before, suddenly the apprehension he'd felt before was, this time, replaced with something else entirely. Resolve. Right then and there, Lew bowed his head.

"Lord, I know you do things in your way and with your timing, but this could not be clearer to me. I have been searching for the direction you wanted my life to take. If it's alright with you, I'd like to tell others about Who You really are."

A peace came over Lew, and he realized what he wanted to do. After a few minutes more in contemplation, he got up, and swiftly walked back over to the table, where Daniel and Audrey, who had finished her browsing, were waiting for him.

Audrey noticed something in his expression, so before Lew could say anything, she asked, "What's up? You look like you found something."

"I did!" said Lew. "I found out what I want to do."

Audrey looked down at his feet and saw the sandals he was wearing.

"Don't tell me you want to be a beach bum!" she said, chuckling a bit.

"Nope. Quite the opposite," he said. "I want to tell others about who the Messiah really is!"

Daniel piped up. "The Messiah? He has yet to appear."

Lew smiled. "Oh, He's appeared. We're just waiting for Him to re-appear."

Audrey smiled, but Daniel frowned.

"Yes, I have heard this story before," said Daniel.

Lew smiled. "Daniel, you live right here where it all happened, and you still haven't seen it. Do you know how fortunate you are? All these sites - all these years! For over 2000 years, people have been coming here, and you have had the privilege of showing things they have only read about. I don't know about everyone else, but if the same thing happens to them that has happened to me, this does not disprove anything. If anything, my faith has been strengthened."

Daniel still had a skeptical look on his face, but Lew could tell his mind had not been changed.

"Thank you for sharing that," said Daniel. Then he paused and said, "Are you ready for the trip to the Sea of Galilee now?"

Lew looked over at Audrey, then as he was turning his head back towards Daniel, he said, "I think I would like to visit another place, if it's OK with you."

"What would this place be?" asked Daniel.

"There is another place that I read about that some say was also a possible site of the Crucifixion. It's called 'Gordon's Calvary'. Do you know where that is?"

"Of course," smiled Daniel. "It is a bus station."

"A bus station!" exclaimed Lew.

"Yes, but I have taken others there before."

"OK, let's go, then," said Lew.

So, they loaded up back in the SUV, and a short time later they pulled up in the parking lot of, sure enough, a bus station. Lew was confused.

"Well, this is not what I expected," he said.

"Yes, I hear that quite often," said Daniel.

Behind the bus station was a small rise, but Lew couldn't see it very well.

"Can you drive around the side so I can see the area from a distance?" asked Lew.

"Certainly," said Daniel, "but I will have to take another side street first."

"That's fine," Lew said as Daniel turned the vehicle around. "I just want to see it from a little further away."

Daniel exited the area, took a couple of turns, then drove around to a street where you could see the side of the hill.

"Stop!" Lew said suddenly. So Daniel pulled over to the side of the road.

"Audrey, look!" said Lew as he pointed at the hill. Sure enough, there was a rock formation on the side of the hill just below a small plateau above it.

"That's it!" Lew said. "That's Calvary!"

CHAPTER 39

2002

Audrey, still looking at the hill, said, "Well, it certainly fits the description."

What Lew couldn't say, was that he had seen this exact site before. In his mind's eye he could see three crosses on the top of the plateau, and on the side was a rock formation that looked just like a skull.

Daniel looked back at Lew, and was fascinated by the look on his face.

"You look as though you have seen this before," said Daniel. It took Lew a few seconds to formulate his response, knowing he had to be careful how he said this without Daniel thinking he was a nutcase.

"When you see the place where the Savior of the world was crucified for no reason other than who He was, you just know," Lew finally said.

They both took a few pictures, then Lew asked Daniel if they could take a walk on the plateau.

"I suppose," said Daniel. "Let me see if I can get us closer."

A few minutes later, the three of them were standing on the very place Lew had seen on his previous excursion. As he held Audrey's hand, he knelt at the place where he'd seen the cross in the middle. Audrey instinctively knelt with him. Lew began to pray.

"Lord, just like Moses, I feel as if I am on holy ground," began Lew. "But as I say that, I realize this place was just another tool you used for your own purposes. I read in the Bible where you cried out to the Father because when you took our sins on Yourself, He turned His back. Thank you for becoming sin, and in doing so, taking the blame and punishment for all we had done and would ever do. I know we will never understand the love that took, but I will live the rest of my life telling others about it."

They both stayed on their knees several minutes, and when Lew finally said, "Amen!", and rose, Daniel had backed off several feet with his hands folded and his head bowed.

"Daniel," said Lew, "I understand there's another place nearby called the 'garden tomb'."

"Yes," said Daniel. "Do you wish to go there as well?"

"Yes, if you don't mind."

"It is a short walk from here," Daniel said. "We can visit it and then return to the vehicle."

"Let's go, then," said Lew and he and Audrey followed Daniel down the rise.

They arrived a short time later at a place called the 'garden tomb'. As they approached a man greeted them with an outstretched hand.

"Hello", said Lew.

"How are y'all doing?" the man asked in a bit of a southern U.S. accent. "I'm Jack."

Lew was a bit taken aback as he shook the man's hand.

"We...we're just fine..." said Lew as he looked at Audrey. "I'm Lewis Donaldson and this is my wife Audrey."

Jack released the handshake, and the man extended his hand to Audrey, who also shook his hand.

"Welcome to the Garden Tomb. Would you like a tour?"

"Yes," said Lew, "but I'm a bit confused. You don't seem to be a local."

Jack laughed and said, "Well, that's because I'm not! My wife and I come over here from our home in Georgia every year during the heaviest part of the tourist season to show visitors around the burial place of Christ. We're both retired, and we spend our time here telling the story of the Garden Tomb. Come on – let me show you."

With that, he and Audrey followed Jack through the outer part of the tomb area as Jack explained the features they saw. The site was really just a cave carved into the side of a massive rock. Then, Jack invited them into the tomb itself. As they walked in, Lew was immediately struck how, just as the Bible had said, they could look through the opening and see the place where Jesus would have been laid.

In his previous 'visit' here, Lew had not actually been to the tomb, so this was the first time he'd actually seen it, and he was a bit surprised at how close it actually was to the crucifixion site. If this was where the body of Christ had been taken, he had not missed it by much. But, then, his mind had been on other things at the time.

Audrey held onto Lew's arm tightly, and as they looked at the interior of the tomb, she whispered to Lew, "I can almost see his body laid here. It feels....holy, I guess"

"That it does," said Lew. "That it does."

"I hear that every day," said Jack. "As far as I'm concerned, it is holy, but not because Christ was buried here – but because He is *not* here!"

Lew saw movement out of the corner of his eye, and he looked and saw that Daniel had followed them into the tomb and was listening to everything they said.

"Yes!" said Lew. "If He was here, hope would be gone!"

"Exactly," said Jack. "Our hope is an *empty* tomb. Let's pray."

Jack led them all in a short prayer that brought tears to their eyes. When he finished, they exited the tomb, and he and Jack exchanged contact information. Then he turned to Daniel.

"If you don't mind, Daniel," Lew said. "I think we'd like to call it a day, and head back to the hotel."

Daniel nodded his head, and they walked back over to the SUV. When they got in, as Daniel was turning the SUV towards the street, he said, "We had tomorrow blocked off as a rest day before we finished up the final day of the tour. Do you still wish to do that?"

"Yes," said Lew. "Let's talk tomorrow about that last day, and we'll go from there."

Daniel nodded, and drove them back to the hotel.

Lew and Audrey were more mentally exhausted than they'd thought they would be at this point, but the day's events had Lew's head in a swirl. Daniel deposited them at the hotel, and they went upstairs to contemplate the day's events. Lew immediately went over to the room's desk, retrieved his Bible, and went over to the bed to do some reading. As he did, it turned out Audrey had done the same thing. For the next couple of hours, they read and discussed the portions of the Scripture they'd just seen for themselves.

Finally, they decided that instead of going out to eat, they would just order room service. Lew was beginning to really miss an 'American' type meal, and there were some items on the menu that helped to satisfy that craving. They spent the rest of the evening discussing the entire trip, and around midnight local time, they drifted off to sleep.

Around nine the next morning, the phone on the bedside table rang. Lew rolled over and picked up the handset.

"Yes?" he said.

"I am sorry to bother you, sir, but would you mind meeting me downstairs? I have something to discuss."

It was Daniel.

"Of course," said Lew. "Can you give me about a half hour to get ready?"

"Whenever you are ready," said Daniel. "I will meet you in the hotel coffee shop."

As he hung up the phone, Audrey said, "Who was that?"

"Daniel," he said. "He wants to talk about something."

"What?" she asked.

"Beats me. You want to come?"

"No, he asked for you, so go ahead," she said. "You can tell me all about it when you get back."

A half hour later, Lew walked through the entrance to the coffee shop and saw Daniel sitting in a corner table in the back. Daniel waived him over, and Lew strode over and sat down.

"Morning, Daniel," Lew said. "What's up?"

Daniel had a cup of coffee on the table in front of him, and he looked down at it while fidgeting with the cup. Finally, he looked back up at Lew.

"I have been doing this for a number of years now," he began, "and I have accompanied hundreds of people to the same sites we visited this week. But, there is something different this time. I cannot shake the feeling that there is something special about you. I have never seen anyone react to some of these places as you have."

He paused, again somewhat nervously fidgeting with the cup.

Finally, he looked up at Lew and asked, "Why are you so sure these stories about these sites are real?"

Lew sat back, trying to decide how to answer that question.

"There is a concept in Christian belief called 'know that you know'," he began. "It means that if you are a believer in and have put your faith in Christ, He will provide the certainty. For a long time, I was not only an unbeliever, I was an atheist. I didn't believe there was such a thing as a 'god'. But, events in my life – very personal events – convinced me to take another look. When I finally decided to accept the truth wherever it took me, that's when the Spirit of God pulled me in, and began to give me the proof. We call it 'faith'. In the Bible, the Apostle Paul defined faith as *'the substance of things hoped for, and the evidence of things not seen'*. I can tell you that I have seen some of those things this week."

Daniel thought about that for a minute, then began.

"All my life this has been a job for me. It was an interesting job, but a job nonetheless. I take people here and say 'this is this', then take them to another place and say, 'this is that'. I take their money, show them all the sites, tell them the stories, give them a good experience, then wait for the next group. It has never been anything other than that. I have considered myself fortunate to be able to meet so many people, tell them all the stories, and make a good living for my family."

"Now, all of a sudden," he continued, looking straight in Lew's eyes, "I am not so sure it is just a story."

Lew smiled. "It's not. Daniel, once you get to that point, If you really want to know the truth, don't stop until you're completely satisfied you've found it. In fact, the Bible says you can 'know the truth, and the truth will set you free', so don't settle!

Daniel thought about that for a moment, then said, "What if I want to pursue this 'truth'? Where would I start?"

Lew smiled. "How about right here?"

"Here?" asked Daniel.

"Yes," smiled Lew. "Right here at this table.....with me."

CHAPTER 40

Second Decade of the 21st Century

Kelly was on her way to the airport again. Since her first trip to Kenya several years ago, she had quickly advanced from her first gig for National Geographic to a hired member of the staff, and then a managing editor. But, with the emergence of digital media, and the decline of published magazines, Kelly saw the handwriting on the wall, and decided to transition away from print publishing to the digital world. Her work at National Geographic had prepared her well for this transition, as she'd been in the middle of their foray into the digital world. But, when Time Magazine began laying off editorial staff, she saw the handwriting on the wall. So, when the offer came from a premier online digital and social media company looking for an experienced photo-editor, Kelly jumped at the chance.

Today, she was flying to Los Angeles along with one of the staff photographers to consult with a client who was interested in enhancing their online presence. They were to do a test layout for the client in hopes of signing them to a management contract. Her management experience, as well as her expertise in the field gave her a nice advantage over whatever competition would be vying for the contract.

They parked in the long term parking lot, and went into the terminal and checked in for their flight, which was scheduled to leave in just over an hour. With time to kill, the photographer accompanying her decided she wanted to look around in the duty free shops in the airport until time to board, so while she was shopping, Kelly decided to just sit in the waiting area. She had been sitting about ten minutes browsing on her phone when a familiar image popped up on the screen and her phone rang.

"Hey sis. What's going on?" she said as she answered the call.

Kelly and her sister had become best friends, and spent time together as much as they could. Neither had families, so they would frequently go shopping together, or maybe just hang out with each other when work wasn't getting in the way.

"Hi, Kelly," came the familiar voice on the other end of the line. "I just wanted to call and see what your schedule looks like for the next several months. I may need your services."

"Okay…" Kelly said with a sly smile on her face. "What do you need photographed?"

"Oh, I don't need a photographer," she said. "I need a maid-of-honor."

It took Kelly an instant for that to sink in, then a wide smile came on her face.

"OH MY GOODNESS, KATIE…" she giggled. "MATT ASKED THE QUESTION!"

Now the giggle came from the other end of the call.

"YES!" Katie said, "and you are my second call."

"I should have been your FIRST call!" Kelly replied in mock disgust. "But, I guess Mom and Dad would have been upset if you'd not called them first. You did call them first, right?"

"Well," said Katie, "Matt kinda gave it away when he asked Dad for permission."

"Ooh, old school. I like it!" said Kelly.

"So?" asked Katie.

"Of course! I can't wait!" said Kelly.

For the next several minutes it was just two sisters talking about wedding cakes, dresses, honeymoon locations, and enjoying the conversation. Before she knew it, the photographer was back, and they were calling her flight.

"Oh, Katie," said Kelly, "They're calling my flight - I have to go. Look, I'll only be gone a couple of days, so as soon as I get back, we're going to find you a dress!"

"You're on!" said Katie, and they said their goodbyes.

As they walked to the gate, Kelly put her phone away and told the photographer the whole story. At least they had something to talk about on the flight now!

CHAPTER 41
Arlington, VA

Second Decade of the 21st Century

> *"There is plenty of security in New York today as a member of the Israeli Knesset, who has emerged as the leader of the coalition to re-establish the Jewish Temple on the Temple mount in Jerusalem, is here to visit family and meet with members of Congress...."*

Tom reached over and turned off the vehicle's radio. With the end of the project in sight, he had lots on his mind, not the least of which was that the team was ready to do a demo for the Military, but CERN had the Supercollider down again for, of all things, a short circuit caused by a weasel that invaded the electrical equipment room and electrocuted itself! When the equipment was restored (and the weasel removed!), there would be another backlog of experiments scientists all over the world were anxious to perform. So they spent their time refining the hardware, software, and preparing a demonstration for the military brass so when CERN gave them access again, they would be ready to make the most of the opportunity.

The decision had been made by Tom, his team, and the upper management at DARPA to present this as an inanimate-only replication process, since the thought of sending exact duplicates of humans through a time portal just presented too many issues, many of which were massively dangerous. It was technically possible – they had proved that – but the dangers overruled the urge to make it happen. Oh well, maybe some time. Just not now. Besides, as he drove Tom's mind had something much larger in his future, as their daughter woke up this morning after she and her friends spent the previous day as her last as a single woman. Today was their daughter's wedding day!

He and Kathy were driving to the Church, wanting to be early since there was still lots to be done before the wedding, and likely both their parents were also on the way over. They arrived and parked in an area they hoped wouldn't get blocked in by the attendees.

"I'm sure Kelly is already here," she told Tom as they exited the vehicle, "so I'm going to go find her and Katie, and make sure everything we did yesterday is perfect."

"Sounds good," said Tom. "I'll check on Brother Bob, then I'll find you guys before the place starts to fill up."

Kathy took off towards the fellowship hall where the reception would be held, and where Katie and Kelly were preparing for the wedding, and Tom headed for the sanctuary.

Tom entered the sanctuary and the only person there was a well groomed man in a suit and tie. "Well, the day is finally here," said Brother Bob as he and Tom met down front where the Pastor was inspecting the place the wedding party would all stand.

"Yes it is," Tom said. "While I'm losing a daughter, I'm gaining a son. Pastor, he's a great guy and a Godly man, so we feel like Katie will be in good hands. Of course, he's going to have to be on his toes. She's a strong young woman, so he'll have his hands full! But, look who I'm talking to. You know all about that, right?"

Bob smiled. "Yes - yes I do! We had many conversations years ago, so I know how strong willed she can be."

"Yes, that's Katie," Tom nodded. "She was so excited when you became pastor here, and there's no one she'd rather have performing the service. We're all grateful for you."

Brother Bob smiled again. "Oh, I am the one who is grateful. I love you guys, and I'm so excited about both Katie and Matt."

Just then, the door to the sanctuary opened, and a man in a dark suit entered and walked up to where they were standing. Tom did a double-take when he noticed the ubiquitous curled tail of a communications earpiece over his left ear.

"Hi", said Brother Bob. "Are you here for the wedding?"

Not smiling, the man said, "I'm here to check security for someone who *is* attending the wedding. Would you please show me the layout? It shouldn't take but a few minutes."

Bob looked over at Tom. Tom shrugged his shoulders, thinking to himself that maybe someone from DARPA decided to attend.

"Sure, may I ask who you're here with?", Brother Bob asked.

"After the review, if you don't mind," said the man. Tom could tell this man was deadly serious, but he said nothing as Brother Bob led him through the adjoining rooms. When they emerged, the man said "Thank you. Just a few minutes, please".

Again, Tom and Brother Bob exchanged glances as the man exited the sanctuary door. A few minutes later, the door opened, and Tom's mouth fell open.

"Dan?" he asked incredulously. "You look just like the picture on your QSL card in my shack!"

Dan strode up to Tom, extended his hand and said, "How are you doing there, Tango Tango?"

As they shook hands, Tom said, "I heard someone from the Knesset was coming into New York today, but I had no idea it was you. How have you been?"

"Great," Dan said, "When you told me a few weeks ago you're daughter was getting married, we had already planned a trip to the States, so I simply arranged my itinerary so I could come by here on the way to my wife's parents. I hope you don't mind the surprise."

"Of course not!" Tom said as he smiled. "I am so pleased you're here. Where's Maddie?"

"She is next door, hopefully talking to Kathy and Audrey," said Dan, who then pivoted and extended his hand to Brother Bob. "Hi Pastor. It is great to see you again."

Bob shook Dan's hand and said, "It's been a while, Daniel. I'm glad you came by to see us. Will you have time for us to catch up after the ceremony?"

"Wait a minute," Tom interrupted. "You guys know each other?"

"Yes, of course," said Dan. "We have known each other almost as long as you and I have been talking on the radio. We met several years ago when he toured Jerusalem, and yes," he continued as he turned towards Bob, "I have a sufficient time window in my schedule, so we can certainly catch up. Tom and I talk regularly via Ham Radio, but you and I have not seen each other since your last trip to Israel."

"Great!" said Brother Bob.

"Tom," said Dan, "it is because of this man I came to know Christ, and his fervor for the faith that let me to getting involved in the Temple project in the first place." Dan paused for a moment, then with a far-away look in his face, said, "It is amazing how God works His will in the lives of men."

As he said that, Brother Bob nodded his head and said, "Amen!"

Tom noticed almost the same look in Brother Bob's face and was going to say something, when just then the wedding coordinator came through the side entrance and told the trio they were ready to begin letting guests in.

"OK," Brother Bob said, then turned to Tom and Daniel. "What do you say we get these two hitched."

Now Tom simply smiled. "Right there with ya', brother!"

Tom had flown the grandparents up from Mississippi and Texas and they were so excited to see their youngest granddaughter tie the knot. Matt had booked a flight to Carmel, California for their honeymoon, and a room at a private B&B that was right on the ocean front. The couple that owned the rental lived nearby, but far enough away that they were assured of privacy. The pictures they'd posted online showed a magnificent view of the Pacific from the cliff where the house was located, so Matt said the exorbitant price he had paid didn't sting so much when he thought of their first days as husband and wife.

The time came. Tom stood with Katie and marveled at how beautiful she was in her wedding dress complete with train. She and Kelly, whom she'd chosen to be her maid-of-honor, had practiced managing that train for when Katie reached the front of the Church. Just before it was time, Tom asked his daughter if she was nervous.

"Not really," she said. "I'm more excited than anything. I've thought about this moment for years, and I just want it all to go right."

"Don't you worry about that, honey," Tom said. "However it goes, even if you fall on your face, you'll look back on this for the rest of your life with a smile. Just enjoy the moment, and let the Lord take care of the rest."

As Tom looked into her face, he knew they would be just fine together. She reached up and gave her dad a kiss on his left cheek, and they both almost lost it right there. Fortunately the wedding director came up right at that moment and told them to get ready.

First the bridesmaids, the flower girl and ring bearer (Kathy's little niece and nephew), and finally, it was time. Katie was beautiful and Tom knew in his heart they would both always remember this moment.

The organist began playing the processional, and the other members of the wedding party marched down the isle and took their places. Then, the bride's march began, the attendees stood, and Tom and Katie began their walk down the aisle.

As they arrived at the altar, Brother Bob opened the ceremony with a small speech on the importance of marriage. Then, he paused for a moment, and a small tear came to the corner of his eye as he looked up at the assembled congregation.

"Every wedding should be a joyous occasion, but I find myself in the enviable position of presiding in this ceremony where the groom is my own son, Matt. So this day is momentous for me as well".

Then, resuming in his 'preacher' voice, he asked the question you hear in every wedding ceremony.

"Who gives this woman to marry this man?" In a strong proud voice, Tom replied, "Her mother and I," then turned and kissed his daughter's cheek, turned to Matt, gave him a firm handshake, then presented Katie's hand for him to take. Tom knew a lot more was said during that service, but this one moment, when he and Kathy entrusted the welfare and happiness of their daughter to such a good young man, Tom instinctively knew they would be just fine.

Finally, the kiss, the presentation, and the march down the aisle together as husband and wife to the applause of all the friends and family who'd come to see Matt and Katie begin their new life together. Kathy mostly held it together during the ceremony, shedding just the right amount of tears as she watched her daughter begin her new life as Matt escorted her down the aisle and out the door.

They held the reception in the family life building adjacent to the Church, took loads of pictures, and had a wonderful time with all those who'd come. Daniel spent most of his time there with Brother Bob catching up, since Daniel had to leave early. Maddie spent her time with Kathy and the Pastor's wife, since she had a similar relationship with them as Tom did with Dan. Tom also spent a few minutes with Dan as he and Brother Bob told the story of how they'd met, but since Tom and Dan talked regularly via Ham Radio, and Tom had others who wanted to congratulate him and his family, it was with Brother Bob that Daniel spent the majority of his time.

Tom was standing with Kathy when Dan came over.

"Tom," he said, "We need to go, since we have so much packed into this trip."

Tom shook Dan's hand, and said, "Thank you both so much for coming. We had no idea you would be here, and we are very honored you chose to make our daughter's wedding one of your stops. This means so much to us."

Kathy and Maddie also exchanged a few last words, then they both walked Dan and his wife over to where Matt and Katie were for them to say their goodbyes. Katie, of course, knew who Dan was, since she'd not only listened to several of their on-air conversations over the years, but had actually spoken to Dan a few times when she would be in the radio shack during one of their contacts.

The time came, and Dan and Maddie left with their security detail, as Tom, Brother Bob, and Kathy waved bye to them. Then they went back into the building where many of the guests were still enjoying themselves.

Finally, it wound down to the time for Matt and Katie to, literally, get out of town. They had a seven p.m. flight, and didn't want to have to rush in the airport, so at a few minutes before four, the wedding coordinator came over and told Tom and Kathy it was time for the couple to go. She and Tom both went over to the happy couple. Katie was talking to Brother Bob so Tom took the opportunity to thank him again for performing the service.

"I know Brother Collins would loved to have performed this service," Tom said when Katie finished what she was saying, "but with Matt as the groom this all worked out so well. Plus, I know Katie has a special place in her heart for you, so I'm glad you are here, and I just want to thank you for today."

"Well, it was all my pleasure, since Katie and I are old friends," he replied.

"Yes, I know," Tom said. "Katie has told me that story several times since you became pastor here."

"In fact, I have a secret I think it's time to tell," Katie said. "You may not remember, Brother Bob, but I left a book in your desk one day after class, but didn't leave my name, because I thought the title might intrigue you. The book was 'Evidence That Demands A Verdict' by Josh McDowell. Do you remember?"

214

Brother Bob's mouth flew open and he had a shocked look on his face.

"That was you?" he all but shouted.

"Yes," she said. "I was afraid you might have assumed it was me!"

"I guess I was a bit preoccupied at the time," Brother Bob said, "and I had a lot going on that day. But, I want you to know how much that book helped me. I had some things going on in my life that led me to Christ, and it was that book that led me to seek the ministry. But it was the insert you placed in the back of the book that made the most difference. Do you remember that insert?"

"Of course I do!" said Katie. "It was a tract called 'The Roman Road', and it contained the short plan of salvation!"

"Exactly!" said Brother Bob. "The 'Evidence' was compelling on its own, but then to run across that simple plan – it was all I needed to finish the trip. After reading it, I prayed to the God I'd denied all those years, and the rest, as they say, is history.

"I'm so glad," Katie said as she smiled, tears welling up in her eyes. "I guess you never know what God will use. Sometimes it's the simple things, and some times it's the extraordinary things."

Brother Bob looked off into the sky as he contemplated that for a moment, then said, "And, sometimes it's both. No one will ever know, or believe, the journey I went through on my way to the Cross."

As Tom observed the look in Brother Bob's eyes, he said, "I'd like to hear that story some time."

"Maybe, Tom," Brother Bob said, "Maybe. But for now, a big blank in my life has been filled in, which makes this day even more wondrous. Besides, you really wouldn't believe it!" he said with a smile. Then, turning to Katie, he said, "Would the bride mind if I gave her a big hug?"

Katie smiled. "Of course not!"

As Brother Bob gave Katie a hug, Tom looked at his watch, then told Matt, "You guys better get a move on. Your flight leaves in just over two hours."

"Right!" he said.

"Let's have a prayer for your travels," Brother Bob said, and he took Katie's hand and offered a quick prayer for their safe trip.

"Katie. I'm proud to know you," he said, when he finished the prayer. "and now you're my daughter-in-law! You two have a great trip, and I'll expect to see you in Church as soon as you get back!"

"You got it!" said Matt as he shook his father's hand, then took Katie by her hand and they went to get their things.

Brother Bob and Audrey joined Tom and Kathy with the rest of the wedding party as they waited for the new couple to come out.

Katie and Matt came to the door, having changed into their 'going-away' clothes. She pitched the ceremonial bouquet to the waiting bridesmaids (Tom had no idea who actually caught it), and strolled down the sidewalk to the waiting limo.

Finally, waving goodbye, they drove out of sight. It had been a great day, but Tom knew Kathy was spent. He was glad Kathy had made arrangements for the wedding coordinator to handle all the clean-up so she didn't have to be concerned about it. Tom found Brother Bob one more time, thanked him, and they left to go home. As he looked back at the Church, Tom thought of all that had happened over the last several years. Now they had yet another memory to add to the mix.

"Come on!" said Kathy. "I'm ready to get out of these shoes."

Tom was sure she was. This had been a long day. Tom turned back towards Kathy, grabbed her hand and gave her a short kiss, and said "Let's go home."

They headed down the sidewalk and walked towards their vehicle. As they did, they passed by the Church's sign facing the road with the welcome information for all to see: "Welcome to Calvary Baptist Church. Robert Lewis Donaldson, Pastor".

-- End --

Author's Note

"A Time And A Place" is the second in the Open Portal series. It's origin came from a dream I had over 25 years ago. However, until the first book in the series, "My Name Is Ben", was created, the means for telling this story eluded me. After completing "My Name Is Ben", this story then began to take place as a Prequel to that book.

If you enjoyed this book, please consider the first book in this series. This first account actually takes place after the events you have just read.

Here is an excerpt from "My Name Is Ben"....

Prologue

The room had been made small and as bland as it could be. The walls were painted an off-white, the single door was plain, constructed of unfinished wood as was the floor, with no paint or varnish. The only lights in the room were two candles on opposite walls. In the center were two benches also of unfinished wood, made simply as one could be and still be called a bench, and between them and off to the side a bit sat a simple small end table. That was it. No pictures, no other furniture - nothing. The entire room was the epitome of the term "nondescript".

The benches faced each other about five feet apart. On one bench sat Thomas Reed. He was dressed much like the room – nondescript. Dark woolen pants, simple black belt, a white cotton shirt, and black semi-dress shoes with black socks. The only other thing he had on him was his wallet in his right back pocket – no pen, no jewelry, no watch – nothing else. Tom had planned this moment for years, so he was understandably nervous and was picking at a place on one of his fingers that he notoriously chewed on when he was thinking. He just sat there waiting.

After about five minutes, he heard five loud beeps on the other side of the door, and he sat up straight with both hands in his lap. Seconds later there was a man standing before him, holding a small walking stick, and looked to be right in the middle of a sentence when the realization set in, then a slow look of bewilderment appeared on his face, and he looked at Tom with shock.

"What has just transpired?"

"Please, sir, sit down," Tom said as calmly as he could, "and I will gladly explain it to you. The first thing you need to know is that you are not in any danger."

The man paused, looked around for a second, then sat down slowly, with an understandable look of concern and yes, fear, but he sat and again said, "Please, I pray you….tell me what has transpired".

"Sir, my name is Tom. Again, you are safe, so try not to be concerned until I have explained the situation to you. First, what is your name?"

The man sighed, folded his hands in his lap and said, "My name is Ben."

The hairs on the back of Tom's neck stood up…..

Acknowledgments

Much of the content of this book came from ideas in conversations with my wife, Amy. Additionally, she aided in the editing of the final draft, as well as contributing to the cover design. It is safe to say this would be a much different book without her contributions.

My daughters, Carly and Lindsay, also contributed to the editing, as well as serving as prototypes, of sorts, for the characters Kelly and Katie. Their support has been amazing as well.

Brother Jerry Lowery was very helpful sharing his experiences on his trip to the Holy Land, and we'd also like to thank Mark Meckler for his encouragement and support of both projects.